THE SEEKER'S JOURNEY

A CONTEMPORARY RETELLING OF PILGRIM'S PROGRESS

MARSHALL DAVIS

TABLE OF CONTENTS

PREFACE

During the fall of 2005, I took a semester sabbatical from my responsibilities as pastor of the First Baptist Church of Rochester, Pennsylvania. For part of that time, I studied at the University of Oxford as a Visiting Scholar. We stayed in a comfortable flat at Regent's Park College, the Baptist hall of this prestigious institution. This was made possible by the Marshall Center of Georgetown College in Georgetown, Kentucky.

The purpose of my stay was to research Baptist origins in England. The Angus Library and Archive at Regent's Park College, as well as the renowned Bodleian Library, were invaluable resources. Two books eventually came out of my time there: *A People Called Baptist: An Introduction to Baptist History & Heritage* and *The Baptist Church Covenant: Its History and Meaning.*

While in Oxford Chris Mepham of the Baptist Union of Great Britain graciously took my wife and me to many sites of historical significance for early Baptists. Among them was the John Bunyan Museum and Library in Bedford. I had read Bunyan's 1678 classic years earlier, but this visit to his home renewed my interest in the classic, as well as Bunyan's other works.

Upon my return to the States I led a study of the classic for my congregation using L. Edward Hazelbaker's version, entitled *The Pilgrim's Progress in Modern English* (1998). Having read older editions of classic, this was a refreshing new translation that made the work accessible to my parishioners. Our church studied the book for months and came away enriched by this great book.

Since that time I have wanted to update Bunyan's book for today's world. There was a time when Pilgrim's Progress was in every Christian home. Often it was the only other book, besides the Bible, that a family owned. Historically it is second only to the Bible in the number of copies published worldwide.

According to Wikipedia, "It is regarded as one of the most significant works of religious English literature, has been translated into more than 200 languages, and has never been out of print. It has also been cited as the first novel written in English."[1]

Although Bunyan's original work is certainly relevant to every age, this great book has declined in popularity among Christians during the last century. The vast majority of Christians in the churches I have served have never read the book. Attempts to retranslate the book into modern English have not solved the problem.

Bunyan wrote in 17th century England, when his Baptist faith was a persecuted minority in England and America. He deals with theological concerns popular in that time and place but which are historical peculiarities today. The world has changed dramatically in the last 340 years. This volume is an attempt to address this concern.

The Seeker's Journey: A Contemporary Retelling of Pilgrim's Progress is not a new translation of the old classic. There have been many other fine attempts to do that. I have used some of them in writing this book. I have already mentioned Hazelbaker's updated version. Another edition I found helpful is *Pilgrim's Progress in Current English* by John Barack (2013). In fact I have used his chapter divisions – for the most part - as the format for my own.

Although my book owes much to Bunyan's work, it is not a translation or an interpretation. This is an original work which seeks to build upon the legacy of the old. It is set in today's world. Although some of the allegorical characters are the same, most of the people and places that my Pilgrim encounters are new. The dialogue is entirely different. The places are renamed. Even the final destination is different. This is not your grandfather's Pilgrim's Progress!

The Seeker's Journey is a humorous exploration of contemporary spirituality. It is an allegorical journey through the landscape of 21st century American Christianity with some obvious and subtle references to modern personalities and authors.

Seeker (who later changes his name to Pilgrim) meets Campus Crusader on his university campus, who instructs him to begin his journey at a lamppost which resembles the one at the boundary of Narnia. Along the Way he falls into the Bog of Existential Angst. He stays in the Town of Therapy for a while. He visits the City of Megachurch where he meets people who sound and look suspiciously like Robert Schuller, Joel Osteen, Rick Warren, and Benny Hinn.

The allegorical characters are still here, but their names are more familiar to modern ears. There is Judgmental, Bored, and Spiritual But Not Religious. Pilgrim meets Tolerant and Intolerant, Sacrament and Tradition, Psychologist and Evangelical. Calvin and Arminius live in a cave overlooking the Valley of Dry Bones.

In the Theologian's House he encounters many interpretations of the Bible and Christ, all of which are recognizable from the American religious landscape – from Creationism to Feminism. Pilgrim visits First Baptist Church where he stays at the home of a Fundamentalist family. He fights the dreaded Apollyon, travels through the Valley of the Shadow of Death, and encounters the Four Horsemen of the New Atheism.

These are just a few of the adventures that Pilgrim and his companion Religious (and then Truthful) have on their journey from their home in the Shadowlands (shades of C. S. Lewis) to their Destination beyond the river. Along the way there are references to Harry Potter, Philip K. Dick, Talladega Nights, and Mark Twain. The ending will surprise you. The Celestial City is not what you expect!

This is a romp through the landscape of contemporary American Christianity that will get you thinking and laughing. I hope that you, the reader, enjoy reading it half as much as I enjoyed writing it.

Marshall Davis
Center Sandwich, New Hampshire
October 2017

PART 1
THE SHADOWLANDS

A loud crack filled the air. His arms shook with the impact that the maul made as it sliced through the log and collided with the chopping block. The sweet scent of sugar maple filled his nostrils. It felt good to get some exercise early in the morning. He had been thinking too much recently about how his parents would react to his announcement, and it had stressed him out. Splitting firewood always helped to clear his thoughts. Even though it was hard work, it was one of his favorite chores around the house.

The screen door to the house creaked open. "It's almost time for breakfast!" his mother called from the house. "Better get cleaned up before you eat and head to school."

"Okay, mom! I'll be right in." Sweat dripped from his curly brown hair. He took off his T-shirt and used it to wipe his face. Then he took long drink from his water bottle and poured the rest of the contents over his head. He had made a decision. Now he had to inform his parents. That was the hard part.

His mother was in the kitchen preparing breakfast. His father was already sitting at the table. "Mom ... Dad ... I need to speak with you." He sat at the table and began. "As you know, I have been struggling at college. I have been so anxious that I cannot concentrate on my studies. But I don't feel ready to go to work fulltime. I need some time to think. So I have decided to take time off from school and travel around the country. Hopefully I will discover who I am and what is important in life. To be quite honest with you, I need to get away. This place has been feeling increasingly dark and dank. It may just be me, but I need to go somewhere brighter."

During the last few months his parents had noticed a change in him and were concerned for his mental health. "We have been talking too," his father replied, "and we think you should see a therapist."

"No! This is not a psychological problem. This is a spiritual problem!"

His mom turned from the stove. "What do you mean 'a spiritual problem'? Oh my God, you haven't joined a cult, have you?"

"No, of course not! It is just that I have been thinking about my life. I need to find some answers before I finish college."

They talked for a while longer, and but it was soon time for him to get to campus. They agreed to continue the conversation later. When Seeker got to campus he decided to skip his first class and talk to the head of the religion department about his dilemma. He made an appointment with the professor and then retreated to the academic quad to wait for the hour to arrive.

Sitting on a stone bench, he began to weep quietly. A man named Campus Crusader came up to him. He had a big black book in one hand and a little pamphlet in the other. Seeker had seen him on campus before but had never talked to him. The man always had the Book in his hand but seemed unable to read from it without the aid of the gospel tract in his other hand.

Campus Crusader asked the man, "Why are you crying?" Seeker replied, "There is an empty space in my heart that nothing can fill. Everything is meaningless. I live in the shadowlands where the sun never shines." Campus Crusader said, "If that is how you feel, why are you sitting here? Why not do something about it?"

"I don't know what to do."

Campus Crusader gave him the gospel tract that was in his hand. On it was written the words: God has a wonderful plan for your life.

"How am I to discover this wonderful plan?" asked the young man.

"Follow the Roman Road described in this pamphlet, and you will be saved."

Crusader pointed, "Do you see that narrow gate in the distance?"

"No, I don't," replied Seeker.

"Well then, do you see that lamppost through the woods?"

"I think I do. It is right beyond that wooden shed, isn't it?" replied the man.

"Correct. Keep your eyes on that light, and you will find the gate. Enter there."

Without further thought of classes, appointments or parents, the young man immediately began to run to the gate. He had not gone far when he heard his parents calling to him. They were running after him, calling him to return. They said they had just made an appointment for him with a good psychiatrist. Seeker put his hands over his ears and ran toward the light, crying out, "Further up, and further in!" Without looking back, he ran as fast as he could toward the lamppost.

TOLERANT AND INTOLERANT

He ran past his neighbors' houses. Some ignored him. Others called 911 to report a man acting suspiciously, possibly a terrorist. Two of his neighbors chased him, calling him to return. One was named Tolerant and the other Intolerant. They would not stop pursuing him. Seeker stopped and asked them, "Why are you chasing me?"

"To convince you to come back with us."

"No I will not return! We live in the Shadowlands, and we hardly know we exist. Sooner or later we will die and be forgotten. I am afraid that one morning, I will wake up and find myself dead, having never really lived.[2] I want more out of life than that. This is why I am leaving. Why don't you come with me?"

"What?" said Intolerant, "And leave behind our opinions and our convictions?"

"Yes, that is exactly what I am suggesting. What you have are nothing more than worldviews inherited from others who live in the Shadowlands. I am looking for more."

"What are you seeking, if it is not a point of view?" asked Intolerant.

"I am seeking Reality."

"And what is Reality?"

"Reality is that which, when you stop believing in it, doesn't go away,'" [3]

"An interesting concept," said Tolerant. "Come back with us, and we will discuss this further."

"Yes," added Intolerant, "We could sponsor a series of debates at the university!"

"Good try!" replied Seeker, "but I am no longer interested in academic debates and discussions. I am looking for Reality."

"We are getting nowhere," Intolerant said to Tolerant. "Let's turn around. It is clear that this man is unreasonable. He is nothing more than a religious fanatic."

"But what if what he's right? What if there is more to life than the Shadowlands? I am thinking about going with him."

"What? Are you crazy? Listen to me. This man is obviously mentally unstable. He has been brainwashed and now he is brainwashing you. Return with me, and we can continue this discussion in a more sensible setting."

Seeker interrupted, "Or you could come with me. You will discover things not dreamt of in your philosophy."

"Intolerant, I have made up my mind," decided Tolerant, "at least for the time being. I am accompanying Seeker beyond the Shadowlands. Lead the way, young man! You do know the way don't you?"

"I got directions from Campus Crusader. He said we are to head toward that lamppost that is visible in the distance. There we will receive further instructions."

"What are we waiting for? Let's go!" And they started off together.

"Well, I'm going home," grumbled Intolerant. "I will not be party to such misguided thinking."

THE BOG OF EXISTENTIAL ANGST

After Intolerant separated from them, Tolerant and Seeker went on their way.

"Tolerant, I am so glad that you decided to accompany me on my journey. If Intolerant had just opened his mind a little bit, he would not have rejected our quest so quickly."

"Since there are just the two of us now," said Tolerant, "tell me more about this Reality we seek. How can we be sure this Reality is real?"

"In college I learned to use reason and logic. The scientific method is probably a good place to start. First let's make observations about the nature of the world. Then we can ask a question concerning what we observe. Then we propose a hypothesis that explains what we have observed. After that we design experiments to test our hypothesis. If the experiment disproves the hypothesis, then we start all over again with another hypothesis. How does that sound?"

"That sounds exhausting!" complained Tolerant. "What if the experiments prove that a perfectly good idea is not true? Must I reject it?"

"Yes, you must."

"Then I would be no better than my neighbor Intolerant! He is always saying that he knows what is true and that others are wrong! He is so judgmental! You are not suggesting that we judge between truth and falsehood, are you?"

"That is the nature of the process. We are seeking truth. That means we must reject error."

Seeker and Tolerant were so absorbed in their conversation that they did not pay attention to where they were going. Before they knew it they had fallen into a swamp. The name of the swamp was Existential Angst. They wallowed in the quagmire for what seemed like ages, becoming covered with foul-smelling slime from head to foot.

Tolerant cried out, "Seeker, what do we do now?"

"I do not know, and I do not care. All is lost. I am mired in a wasteland of Nothingness and Despair."

Tolerant was indignant. "Is this the Reality that you promised me? Can't you use your scientific method to get us out of here?"

Seeker said nothing. Disgusted with the whole thing, Tolerant made a mighty effort and managed to reach the edge of the bog. He lifted himself out and immediately started back on the path towards home. He did not look back or give a second thought to Seeker, who was sinking deeper into the depths of the bog.

Now Seeker was alone. Even though he knew he was dying, he continued to face the lamppost and try to push forward, but he could not move an inch. Then he noticed a man standing at the edge of the bog. His name was Prozac. He asked Seeker what he was doing in the bog. "I was told to come this way by Campus Crusader," responded Seeker. "But now I have ended up in this bog, dying in despair."

"Why didn't you use the stone steps?" he said, pointing to some stepping stones that traversed the bog.

"I did not see them because I was not looking where I was going. That is how I ended up in this desperate situation."

"Give me your hand," replied Prozac, stretching forth his arm.

He pulled him ashore, set him on firm ground, and urged him to get on with his journey. Seeker asked him, "Why isn't this Bog drained so that seekers do not unwittingly fall into it?"

"This swamp cannot be made into dry land. It is a part of the Reality which seekers seek. Those who search for Truth with all their hearts must come to this bog. Some sit for a while at its edge and contemplate its depths. Then they move on, carefully using the steps that span the swamp. Others dive in headfirst and are never seen again. Still others drink of the waters of the bog and return home to the Shadowlands with the scent of Angst upon them forever. I help some across, and they go on their way. Others come home with me and dwell in my house for their rest of their lives."

After thanking Prozac for saving him, Seeker continued on his way.

Meanwhile Tolerant arrived back in the Shadowlands. His neighbors wanted to know all about his adventure. Some admired him for starting out on the journey. Most called him a fool for leaving home and risking his life on a fool's errand. Others mocked him for only going as far as the Bog. They called him a coward for turning around when the going got tough. His closest friends praised him for his open-mindedness and for rejecting the arrogance of one who pretends to seek Truth. But from that day forward, Tolerant always wondered what might have happened if he had continued on the Way.

PSYCHOLOGIST

Seeker left the bog behind and traveled alone. In the distance he saw a man walking on an adjacent path that would soon intersect with his. At the crossroads he greeted the man, whose name was Psychologist. He lived in a town called Mental Health, a large community not far from the Bog. This man had heard of Seeker's adventure, since it had become common knowledge in the scientific community.

Psychologist eagerly engaged him in conversation. "I can see that you are quite troubled. Would you like to talk about it?"

"You are right. I am burdened," answered Seeker, "How did you know?"

"I am a friend of Prozac, who helped you escape from the Bog of Angst."

"Are you? Please thank him for me. He saved my life."

"I will do that next time I see him. But I see that you are still in distress. Tell me how you are feeling."

"I am embarrassed to say, but I feel burdened by shame and guilt. I have done terrible things in my life, and I feel like I cannot talk about these things with anyone."

"Will you take my advice?"

"Seeing that you are a friend of Prozac, who helped me when I was in great need, I will gladly listen to you."

"I advise you to free yourself from this terrible burden. It will take some time. You will have to delve into your childhood and plumb the depths of your upbringing. But I am confident that in time you can be free from all guilt. You will never be able to reach your full potential until you do."

"That is what I desire above all! It is one of the reasons I embarked on this journey."

"Who told you that the path you are traveling would lead to freedom from guilt?"

"Campus Crusader told me that if I followed the Roman Road then all my sins would be forgiven."

"Damn him!" shouted Psychologist. "That man does not know the remedy for guilt! His religion is the cause of guilt! First he places an unbearable burden of moral demands on people's hearts. When people cannot live up to them, he sells them his spiritual snake oil, promising that it will free them from the burden. I advise you to stay clear of him at all costs."

"But this burden of guilt feels very real, and I felt it long before I met Campus Crusader."

"Tell me, when did you first begin to feel this burden?

"When I went to church and heard the Book preached."

"That is exactly the problem! In my practice I have come across many people with the same affliction. People are conditioned by religion from an early age, and it causes them much distress later in life. The most common symptoms are guilt and shame."

"All I know is that I desire to be free of these feelings."

"You do not need to travel this road in order to be free of your burden. I can show you a better way, a scientific way."

"That is exactly what I am looking for. Please, show me this way."

"In the next village there is a man whose name is Therapist. He is a very caring fellow with a good reputation in the community. He has the training and skill to remove this burden from your heart. I advise that you make an appointment with him immediately. His office is only a mile from here. If he is not available, you can make an appointment with his daughter Counselor. She is nearly as good as her father. After a few sessions, you will notice a difference in your life. Then you can return to your home and the university. Before you know it you will have a family of your own, a well-paying job, and be a well-balanced member of society."

Seeker thought about Psychologist's words. *If this man's words are true – and they certainly sound true – then it would be wise to follow his advice. After all, his friend Prozac, did save my life. I guess it would not do any harm to give it a try.* Seeker decided. "What is the address of this Therapist?"

"Good choice! You won't regret this. He is at 1000 Hill Street. See that hill in the distance? His office is in the first building on the left."

THE TOWN OF THERAPY

So Seeker left the path and entered the Town of Therapy. He made an appointment with Therapist for the next day. He found an apartment in town and settled in. At first he saw Therapist twice a week and then once a week.

But it seemed like the more he talked to Therapist, the more things he uncovered from his past to feel guilty about. Instead of alleviating this guilt, the sessions seemed to compound it. After months of talking, Seeker began to think that Psychologist's promise of freedom from his burden was mistaken. He was sorry that he had taken his advice and turned aside from the Road.

One day when Seeker was taking a stroll on the outskirts of the town he ran across Campus Crusader. Immediately he blushed with shame.

"Aren't you the man I found crying on a bench in the Shadowlands?"

"Yes, I am."

"What are you doing here? I set you on the path to the gate which is near the lamppost."

"Yes, you did."

"Then why have you turned aside and left the Way?"

"I fell into the Bog of Angst. Prozac saved me. Then I met his friend Psychologist, who convinced me that the best way to be released from my burden of guilt was by entering this town and seeing a man named Therapist."

"What did this Therapist say?"

"He did not say a lot. He mostly asked questions about my parents and my feelings. When he did speak, he said I was making good progress, and soon I would be free from guilt and shame. I also spoke to him about you, your Book and your pamphlet. He said that if I was really interested in spiritual matters that I should follow the Road Less Traveled.[4] He said it is one of the few spiritual paths that worked. But recently I have come to the conclusion that Therapist is unable to help me any further. He has done as much as he can. He has given me insight into my heart and mind, but I fear he knows nothing more than the workings of the brain."

"Is that really all you want? To live a well-adjusted life? If that is what you desire, then by all means stay here and learn from Therapist. Then return home to the Shadowlands. But if you desire to move beyond the shadows to a life of greater meaning and purpose, then – I urge you - return to the Road."

Campus Crusader took out his Book and began to read. As Seeker listened to the words, his heart began to feel things that could not be described. He realized that he had to immediately leave Therapy and get back on the Road.

"Sir, I have turned aside from the Way. Am I allowed to return and continue my journey?"

"Everyone is always welcome on the Road."

Without looking back, contacting his landlord, or retrieving any of the self-help books he had purchased, Seeker immediately left Therapy and resumed his journey on the Road. Campus Crusader gave him a big hug, and sent him on his way with his blessing. But he kept a watchful eye on Seeker until he disappeared over the first hill.

PART 2
BEYOND THE GATE

Seeker walked quickly – trying to make up for lost time. He did not greet any of his neighbors from the Town of Therapy, even if they asked him a direct question. He was afraid that he might be delayed or tempted to return. After a few miles he reached the Gate. By the light of the nearby lamppost he could read the words over the gate: "Know Thyself."

He was about to step through the gate when a man suddenly appeared. He was an older man, short and stocky, with a long beard, snub nose and bulging eyes. His name was Sincerity. He stared at Seeker intently.

"Who are you? Where are you from? What do you want?"

Seeker replied, "I am a poor wayfaring stranger, traveling through this world of woe.[5] I come from the Shadowlands, and I am headed toward the Bright Land. I was told that to reach my destination that I must pass through this Gate. Will you step aside, so that I can enter?"

"I will gladly allow you to pass," replied Sincerity. "But first I need to ask you a question. Do you know yourself?"

"What kind of a question is that? I already told you my name, where I was from and where I am going!"

"Yes, but do you know yourself?"

Seeker was thoughtful for a moment. "If I truly knew who I was I would not have come on this journey. I seek to discover the answer to that question."

"Good answer!" And he opened the gate. As Seeker was about to step through, Sincerity suddenly pulled him back.

"Why did you do that?"

"Sniper," replied Sincerity. "In that ivory tower in the distance there is a militia under the command of a man named Post-Modern. He opposes anyone who believes that anything is true. His snipers will shoot at anyone who passes through this gate.

"Ah, yes. I met some of them at the university. Thanks for the warning."

"By the way, who told you to enter by this gate?"

"Campus Crusader."

"Then I will help you pass safely through the door. But first, why did you come alone? Don't you have family or friends who could accompany you?"

"No, my parents, friends and neighbors thought I was foolish to embark on this journey. My parents wanted to send me to a psychiatrist to convince me to abandon this quest."

"Did any of them follow you?"

"Yes, two of my neighbors – Tolerant and Intolerant - chased me in order to persuade me to return home. I convinced one of them – Tolerant – to come with me for a while."

"Why is he not with you now?"

"We both fell into the Bog of Angst. That was too much for him. As soon as he got out he went home, whereas I continued on my way."

"Too bad. Does Truth mean so little to him that he was not willing to endure suffering to find it?"

"To be honest with you," said Seeker with a grimace, "I am no better than he. As soon as I got out of the bog I turned aside from the road to spend some weeks in the Town of Therapy.

Psychologist convinced me that it was a better way to free myself from guilt and shame."

"Oh, so you met Psychologist! He is a very persuasive fellow, and a very good listener. Undoubtedly he referred you to Therapist or Counselor."

"Yes he did. And I spent much time and money on therapy."

"Did it help?"

"Yes, it helped. But in time it became clear that it was like peeling back the layers of an onion. There is no end to the process. I could have spent the rest of my life in Therapy and never have succeeded in being entirely free of guilt."

"Very good! If you learned that lesson, then it was worth the time and money. Most people spend their lives simply trying to adjust to the Shadowlands instead of seeking a better country."

"I am grateful for what I learned in therapy and for seeing that it has its limits."

"Speaking of limits, let me tell you about the path that you are about to travel beyond the gate. Look through the gate. What do you see?"

"I see a narrow way."

"Correct. The Way is narrow. It is the Ancient Way, established from the foundation of the world. Holy men and women have traveled this path for generations. Now it is your turn, if you are willing."

"I am willing. But now that I look closely at the Gate, I see that it is very small, barely wide enough for me to squeeze through."

"Yes, the Gate is strait and the Way is narrow. One person can barely pass through the opening. No one can enter with another at his side. Furthermore you can bring nothing with you - neither your possessions nor family nor friends. Most important you can carry with you neither your sins nor your good works."

"How am I to leave them behind?"

"All you need to do is enter through the Gate. It will do the rest."

"How about my guilt and shame? Will it remove them as well?"

"That must wait for the Hill of Deliverance. You will be able to lay down that burden later."

Seeker proceeded through the Gate, keeping a watchful eye on the Sniper's ivory tower. Sincerity called after him, "Remember to keep asking questions. Do not settle for answers without examining all the possibilities. If you are not willing to examine everything, then you might as well not be on the journey. The unexamined life is not worth living."

Seeker waved goodbye to the gatekeeper. As he waved, he noticed some words over the rear of the Gate. It read: "The Way, the Truth, and the Life." Sincerity called out some final instructions, "After you have traveled a few miles, you will see the house of the Theologian. Knock at his door, and it will be opened unto you. He will help you to understand your new life." With those words of encouragement and warning, Seeker began to travel the narrow way.

THE THEOLOGIAN'S HOUSE

He continued along the path until he reached the house of the Theologian. Beside of the door was a sign that read, "Ask, and it will be given to you; seek, and you will find; knock, and it will be opened to you." So he knocked, but there was no answer. He knocked again, and still there was no response. He kept knocking, and finally the door was opened. A distinguished gentleman stood before him, wearing a tweed jacket with elbow patches and smoking a pipe.

"Sir," said Seeker, "I am a pilgrim on this strait and narrow way. The gatekeeper told me to come to your house, and you would teach me about the Way."

The Theologian responded, "Enter in, and I will show you things that will be helpful to you."

THE PASTOR'S PORTRAIT

He escorted him into his private study. The first thing that Seeker noticed was a portrait hanging on the wall. The man in the picture was dressed in a clerical robe with a liturgical stole around his neck and three velvet bands on the arms. Behind him was a wall of books – science and history books on one side, religious and philosophical books on the other. Framed diplomas adorned the wall. The man was holding the Book in one hand a newspaper in the other. A tear glistened on his cheek, but his eyes were set like steel. His brow and hands bore scars like the Lord's.

"Who is the man in this picture?" asked Seeker.

"He is one who has read a thousand books and felt a thousand sorrows. He studies long and works hard, but not as the world works. He counsels others and bears their burdens. He is a Pastor. His work is to proclaim the good news, ask the right questions, and communicate the wisdom of the ages. I am showing you his portrait so that you will recognize him if you encounter him on your journey. There are many on the path who pretend to be pastors, but they are not. They proclaim only what they have heard, but not what they know. Flee from them."

"Campus Crusader proclaimed good news to me, but he does not look like this man. He told me that God had a wonderful plan for my life."

"Campus Crusader is not a Pastor. He is an evangelist. Though he is often found on college campuses, he distrusts any learning that disagrees with his beliefs. He praises the Book and reads from it, but he is unable to interpret the Book without a pamphlet to guide him. He knows little and seeks to know little more. The little he knows is not untrue, but neither is it True. His message is sufficient to point seekers to the Gate, but it cannot guide them beyond the Gate. Although he is mature in years, he thinks like a child. When one passes through the Gate, one must leave behind childish things. He is unwilling to do that. He guides people to the Gate, but he is unwilling to travel beyond it. If you continue on the Way, you will not see him again."

"Does that mean that one must have much education to be a pastor?"

"No, there are fine pastors with little formal education. But their advice is imperfect because their knowledge is imperfect. They do not know what they do not know. Therefore they are unable to guide others into the Unknown. You will encounter them on the road. Treat them as brothers, but we be cautious of their advice. They will insist that you stay with them at some wayside chapel, saying that it is too dangerous to continue further. Do not listen to them. Brave all dangers and continue to the end."

"But what about the apostles of our Lord? They were unlettered men."

"That is true. Most of the apostles could neither read nor write because that was the age in which they lived. Does that mean that we should not learn to read and write? Of course not! Would you be better off if you could not read the Book? Are you better off if you never study the origins and history of the Book? Ignorance is not a virtue. The more we know, the better we understand the Book, and the more useful we are to the Lord. Beware of pastors who belittle learning yet claim to know what the Book means. Come, and I will show you the many ways that the Book can be interpreted."

THE SHRINE OF THE BOOK

Theologian took him by the hand and led him into a large rotunda. In the center of the room was the Book laying open on a pedestal, illuminated from above by a stained glass dome in the roof. There were twelve semicircular chapels that branched off the central chamber. They were small and dark. In each of the chapels was a man or woman with a copy of the Book.

When he looked closely he saw that each of the copies bore a different cover. In one chapel there was a gilded Book perched on an altar, and on the altar was the word Bibliolatry. A man was kneeling before the Book. In another chapel a man was waving a copy of the Book and preaching loudly at those who walked by his chapel. On his Book were written the words "Inerrant & Infallible." In the third chapel was a man holding scissors. With them he was cutting out the parts of the Book that he deemed contradictory and unscientific. Most of the Book lay in shreds on the floor, and what was left was impossible to read.

In the fourth alcove was a woman. The Book in her hands bore the subtitle "Myths and Fables." The fifth recess had a woman at a lectern reading from the Book. On a blackboard behind her were written the words "The Bible as

Literature." The sixth chapel was empty except for a copy of the Book locked in a glass case on the wall. A small hammer used for breaking the glass hung beside it. On the glass was emblazoned the words: "Open Only in Case of Emergency."

The seventh chapel had a man scowling while reading from the Book. The cover of his Book bore only the numerals 1611. Seeker peered into the next chapel and saw a woman in clerical robes. She held a Magic Marker in her hand. With it she was marking out all masculine pronouns and references to God as male. On the cover of her Book were the words "Hagia Sophia."

The adjacent chapel looked like a museum. On one side was a replica of Noah's ark with tiny animals marching in two by two. On the other side was an exhibit of the Garden of Eden depicting dinosaurs frolicking with human children. The man curating this exhibit bore the name of one of Noah's sons. In his hand was a copy of the Book, but something about the Book didn't look right. Upon closer examination Seeker noticed that the first few pages of the Book were much larger than the rest of the book. These same pages were dog-eared with wear, whereas the rest of the book was only lightly worn. On the cover of the book was the number 4004.

The copy of the Book in the next chapel looked similar. But in this edition the final pages of the Book were oversized and worn. Pasted on the sides of this room were charts and timelines. Colorful images of multi-headed beasts populated the walls. There were numbers and calculations scratched on blackboards. Among them were the numbers 1000, 666, 144, 40, 7 and 3½. A man with a crazed look in his eyes handed him a tract, which instantly burned Seeker's hand. He dropped it immediately and ran on.

The neighboring chapel was very different in tone. Red and pink hearts decorated the walls. Pleasant music wafted through the air, mingling with an aroma that smelled like cotton candy. Everywhere he looked the word LOVE was plastered on the wall. The woman in his chapel read from a very thin Bible, which looked like most of it had been edited out. On the cover of her Book were the numbers 3:16.

Seeker had come full circuit. The final chapel in the rotunda was empty. It had the feel of an abandoned storefront which had once housed a bustling enterprise. Scraps of paper lay scattered on the floor amidst dust and dirt. Seeker noticed a ragged paperback edition of the

Book with a ripped denim cover tossed into a corner. He picked it up. On the cover was the word "Paraphrase." Seeker returned it to the floor, wiped the dust off his hands, and walked back into the central chamber of the great room.

"What is this place?" Seeker asked Theologian.

"This is the Shrine of the Book, which honors the inspiration and authority of the Holy Scriptures."

"But why are there so many chapels and different editions of the Book?"

"That is because there are many approaches to reading – or not reading – the Book."

"Which one is right?"

Theologian was quiet for several moments and then replied sadly, "All think they are right."

"But which one has the true copy."

"That is the problem. We do not have any original manuscripts of the Book. They were lost long ago. What you see here are translations of copies of revisions. Furthermore there is no agreement concerning which smaller books should be included in the Book. Look beneath the Book in the center."

Seeker looked, and saw that the pedestal upon which the Book was perched was actually a bookcase. In the bookcase were dozens of other books. They bore names he recognized like Enoch, Barnabas, Judith, Adam, Philip, Thomas, and Magdalene. There were volumes in Greek, Latin, Hebrew, Syriac, and Coptic. Other volumes bore the titles Apocrypha and Pseudepigrapha.

"What are these books," Seeker asked.

"These are books that are no longer in the Book."

"Why are they not in the Book?"

"Men decided long ago that they were not worthy, but not everyone agreed."

"This is confusing to me," admitted Seeker. "How am I to know which edition of the Book to read? How am I going to interpret it correctly? Before I came into your house it was simple. If the Book said something, I believed it. But now I am not sure what to believe."

"Doubt is the beginning of wisdom," replied Theologian. "Only the ignorant are certain. Truth is not easy to discern, but do not be discouraged. When one learns the history of the Book's writing, transmission, collection, and interpretation, then truth will become apparent.

But I warn you, many will not like what you discover. They prefer to read their own copy of the Book in the darkness of their private chapels. They pretend that their copy is the only Book and their interpretation is the only correct interpretation. It is tempting to hide in such a chapel, but you must remain in the center and in the light."

THE GALLERY OF CHRISTS

Next Theologian led Seeker into a hallway that seemed to go on forever. On the walls hung framed pictures of Christ. Other halls branched off the main hallway in a seemingly endless maze.

"How can this be?" Seeker asked Theologian. "From the outside, your home looks like a small English cottage, but inside it holds a large rotunda and a dozen chapels. Now I see that it branches into huge art gallery."

"Have you ever read the Harry Potter books?" inquired Theologian. Seeker was surprised at the question. The religious people he had known in the Shadowlands frowned upon the reading of such literature. They said that such books condoned witchcraft, which was forbidden by the Book.

Cautiously Seeker admitted, "Yes, I have. I enjoyed them very much."

"Good for you! There is more Truth hidden in the tales of Hogwarts than in many theological tomes. Do you remember the Undetectable Extension Charm?"

"Yes, I do. It is a spell that extends the internal dimensions of something without affecting the external dimensions. The trunks of Hogwarts students bore those charms so they could hold all their possessions. Cars and tents often had those charms. I remember when Hermione used the charm on her handbag to carry everything she needed."

"Exactly!" said Theologian. (At that moment Seeker thought that Theologian looked a little like Dumbledore.) "Where do you think Joanne Rowling got that idea?" Without giving Seeker a chance to respond, Theologian blurted out, "She got it from me! She once stood right where you are standing now. And she was not much older than you. Now look carefully at these portraits on the wall."

Seeker looked at the portraits of Christ that hung on the wall. "They are moving! Just like the portraits at Hogwarts!"

"Correct! This is where she got the idea."

Seeker walked slowly through the halls of the gallery examining the paintings. There were hundreds of Christs. Some of the pictures Seeker recognized from church and Sunday School. Sallman's *Head of Christ* smiled serenely as he walked past. Even as a child Seeker had thought it strange that Jesus had pale skin and light brown hair. How could you spend all your time outdoors and not get a tan? Furthermore most of Middle Easterners that Seeker had seen in photos had much darker skin and hair than the Sunday School Christ. Would not Jesus have looked like them?

The pictures of Christ went on and on. Many of them looked very different than the Jesus Seeker had seen in picture books or films. One showed Christ with a kippah on his head and payot hanging on either side of his face. Another frame could barely contain a Jesus with fiery eyes warning Seeker of the apocalypse to come. "The Son of Man is coming in our lifetime!" yelled this Jesus. Seeker quickly moved out of reach of the portrait.

The next portrait was an African Jesus wearing dreadlocks and a crown of thorns. Another depicted Jesus standing by the seaside laughing. Seeker stood for a long time before this one. He had never thought of Jesus laughing before. But in this Hogwarts style portrait, Jesus laughed in such a natural and infectious manner that Seeker found himself laughing aloud with him. He finally had to move on to catch his breath.

In the next hallway there was a female Christ, an Asian Christ, a Native American Christ, and a Hispanic Christ. The paint of the Transgender Christ was still wet. In one picture Jesus wore a black leather jacket and rode a Harley. "That is a bit much," thought Seeker. In another picture Christ's body was covered in tattoos, and he wore a Mohawk.

In one picture Christ looked like Che Guevara and held a copy of Das Kapital in his hand. In another he was a soldier with an automatic weapon slung over his shoulder. When Jesus began discharging his weapon in the direction of the hippie Jesus across the hall, Seeker hurried out of that hallway and sought a quieter section of the gallery.

He found an area that looked to be the oldest section of the house – well over a thousand years old. These pictures of Christ looked more like icons than paintings. Plus they did not move. That was a relief to Seeker, who had enough of Jesus staring and yelling at him. In one image Christ looked like any ordinary man. In another he appeared like a god. In a third he was walking on a beach but left no footprints. In a fourth image Christ was so transparent as to be barely visible.

Seeker came upon a pair of portraits that hung side by side. They were identical in every way that he could tell, even to a Greek word printed in the bottom right corner of the portrait. After much searching Seeker finally discovered the difference between the two. In one the Greek word was homoousios and in the other it was homoiousios. Only an iota distinguished them. A plaque beside the pictures explained that the difference between the two portraits is a matter of life and death.

Seeker shook his head and moved on. In the next hall there was a two headed Christ, a three-headed Christ, and a seven-headed Christ. In another Christ was pictured as a Lion and in another a Lamb. One portrait depicted Jesus as an angel with wings. Another was a wedding photo of Christ and Mary Magdalene. Judas Iscariot was standing beside him as his best man.

One room in the gallery was devoted to how Jesus became God. Some portraits depicted Jesus becoming divine at his baptism. Another at his resurrection. A third at his birth. A fourth before his birth. One contemporary portrait was given a prominent place on a wall all by itself with a prie-dieu before it. It was a picture of the baby Jesus laying in a manger with a halo around his head. The carpet around this picture was very worn and spotted with drippings from candle wax. A plaque under the picture identified him as the Talladega Jesus.[6]

"I've had enough of this!" said Seeker out loud. He went to find Theologian, who was pondering the Homoousios Twin Jesuses. "What is this place? Why are there so many strange pictures of Jesus? None of them looks like the real Jesus to me."

"You are correct," replied Theologian. "None of these are the real Jesus."

"Then why are you showing them to me?"

"Because the best way to know the real Jesus is to know who he is not. Many people worship these Christs. They believe wholeheartedly in them. For them they are real. But in reality they are phantoms of their imaginations."

"Then who is the real Christ?"

"That is the right question!" replied Theologian with a smile. "Now we can go on to the next part of my house."

"Aren't you going to answer my question?" responded Seeker irritably.

"No, I am not here to give you answers. I am here to help you ask the right questions. Didn't Sincerity explain that to you at the Gate?"

Yes, but I want the answer!" demanded Seeker. "Who is the real Jesus?"

"Correct!" responded Theologian.

"Correct?" shouted Seeker.

"Yes. That is the correct question. The Way of Christ is about asking the right questions, not having the right answers. The pilgrim who goes furthest on the Road is the one with the most unanswered questions who will not tolerate unquestioned answers."

THE MATHEMATICIAN'S CUBICLE

Theologian escorted Seeker through a glass door out of the gallery and into another room. The walls were covered with whiteboards and blackboards. Freestanding glassboards were positioned around the room. The boards were covered in mathematical calculations. Most were far beyond Seeker's understanding. (He had never been good at math in school.) Theologian explained that these equations had to do with quantum physics, the Big Bang and the fabric of the universe. Another board described the speed of light and its relationship to time. One blackboard caught Seeker's eye. It held two simple equations that Seeker could understand. One was 1+1=1. The other stated 1+1+1=1.

"Surely whoever wrote those equations has made a mistake," Seeker said to Theologian. "Even I know that 1+1=2 and that 1+1+1=3."

"You are thinking in earthly terms," Theologian explained. "These equations have to do with theology. Divine mathematics are as different from human mathematics as Newtonian physics is from quantum physics. These equations describe Christ and God."

"What do they mean?"

"They do not mean anything! That's the whole point."

"I don't understand."

"Exactly! Now you've got it!"

THE APOLOGISTS

Theologian guided Seeker through the house, out a back door, and into a garden. The sun was shining and the air smelled fresh. The peace and quiet of the garden was a great relief to Seeker after the noise of the rotunda and the gallery.

The first thing that Seeker noticed was a set of three life-size statues. They depicted three ministers – all men - standing next to each other. They were human, but they had a decidedly simian appearance. They reminded Seeker of the film *Planet of the Apes*. One of the ministers covered his eyes with his hands, one covered his ears, and the third covered his mouth.

"The detail in these statues is amazing!" commented Seeker, as he bent to examine the statues closer. All of a sudden the one he was examining blinked, causing Seeker to jump back in alarm. "They are alive!" he exclaimed.

"Yes," replied Theologian, "but barely."

"Who are they?"

"They are three ministers. Years ago they knocked on my door, just like you did. They saw the same things that you have seen, but they were not able to accept what they had seen and heard. They went into a panic, stumbling all over each other trying to get back to my front door, but they could not find it. Eventually they found this door to my garden. Soon after they got into the sunlight they froze in the positions you see them in today. Now they forever "see no evil, hear no evil, and speak no evil."

"What do you mean?"

51

"They were not able to accept that the Book had a history of development. The idea that it contained contradictions and errors frightened them to the depths of their being. So they pretended it was not so. They developed elaborate theories to explain the contradictions. They concluded that there only appeared to be errors and contradictions. Also the historical fact that the Christian understanding of Christ developed over the centuries shook their faith. They physically shook at the thought.

They agreed among themselves that they would pretend that my house did not exist, and that the things they heard here were not real. They convinced each other that my house was an illusion – a work of the Enemy. They took to calling themselves Apologists, explaining to people who came out of my house that it was a dangerous breeding ground for heresies. They refused to change their minds. In time they froze into the positions that you see them in today. They have moved barely an inch in the decades they have stood here."

A shiver went down Seeker's spine at the thought that ministers could be so afraid of Truth. He quickly moved to another part of the garden.

Faith and Works

A little further along the garden path was a playground where two children were playing on a seesaw. One was a boy, and one was a girl. You could tell from their appearance that they were siblings, although the boy looked somewhat older. As they teetered back and forth, the two were squabbling, as children often do. Each was insisting that they were the favorite of their Father. They went so far as accusing each other of being illegitimate children.

"Who are these children?" inquired Seeker.

"The girl's name is Faith," explained Theologian, "and the boy is Works. They spend all their time on this teeter-totter, going back and forth. Each tries to go higher than the other. Each tries to bump the other off their seat by hitting the ground as hard as they can."

"Why are they fighting? Can't they just get along?"

"You would think they could. They are siblings after all. But for some reason they have a hard time understanding each other. They have very different personalities, much like their cousins Mary and Martha, who live down the road."

"Why don't their parents intervene?"

"Their Father and their mother, whose name is Grace, insist that both Faith and Works are their beloved children. They see nothing wrong in their bickering. In fact they take pleasure in it. They say it makes for a lively household."

Theologian took Seeker by the arm and led him down the garden path toward a hedge that bordered the property. Beyond the hedge Seeker could see a hill, and on the hill was a Cross. As soon as he saw it two things happened. First he felt the urgent need to approach the Cross without delay. Second, the guilt and shame that he had momentarily forgotten about while at the Theologian's house came back in full force.

"I am sorry to cut short my visit to your house," said Seeker. "But I must continue my journey at once. The sight on the hill in the distance calls to me."

"That is the way it should be. But remember the things you have learned here. They will protect you from many dangers on the road. Know also that the things you saw at my house are only things of the mind. The Way has to do with the heart, soul, and strength as much as the mind. Go now, and may the Comforter go with you."

Seeker jumped the hedge like an athlete jumping a hurdle and made his way toward the hill. He glanced back to wave goodbye to Theologian, but the house was gone. He saw the gate in the distance and the road he had traveled. The hedge, which he had just jumped, was still there. But where Theologian's house had stood was only an empty field ... with three statues standing by themselves.

Part 3

Calvary

There was a tug at his sleeve and a sharp pain on his arm. The thorns that bordered the road to the Cross snagged his shirt and pierced his skin. He instinctively moved to the right to avoid the bush and felt a sharp nip on his other arm. The road was becoming more constricted. "Strait and narrow," he thought, just as the gatekeeper had said. As he continued on his way up Mount Calvary, his breathing became heavier. He could hear his heart thumping in his chest due to the steepness of the grade.

He hiked more slowly and carefully. Eventually the way became so narrow that he had to turn sideways to avoid the briars. As he approached the tree line the bushes decreased in height, which gave him more arm room. As he came over a rise he saw the rocky summit. On it stood his destination. His heart rejoiced and a wide grin crossed his face as he ran the rest of the way, dropping in exhaustion at the foot of the Old Rugged Cross. A wave of love flowed over him. His guilt and shame were gone in an instant, as if a physical burden had been removed from his back.

He lay on the ground before the Cross weeping in joy and relief. Then he noticed that a bright light surrounded him. Wiping his tears he saw three Shining Ones. They greeted him by name. One of them said, "Your sins are forgiven." The second told him to remove his clothing, which had become ragged and torn from the journey. In their place he offered Seeker a new set of traveling clothes.

The third one touched his forehead with his hand. It burned, and Seeker could tell immediately that it left a permanent mark. But when he felt for a scar, his forehead was smooth. With the other hand the Shining One reached into Seeker's chest and – to Seeker's amazement - removed his heart. Seeker saw that it was as hard and cold as stone. It was replaced with a new heart, upon which had been written his new name, which no one knew but himself. The way to the Celestial City was also written on his heart.

"What should people call me now?" he asked the Shining One. "They cannot call me by my real name, for no one knows it. And my old name is no longer true."

"You must pick a name by which you will be called on earth."

"I shall no longer be called Seeker, but Pilgrim."

The Shining Ones nodded their heads in approval and disappeared. Pilgrim leaped into the air for joy and continued on his way.

THE SLEEPERS

He descended the hill and came to the bottom of the other side. Pilgrim saw what looked like a field of stones with a wooden bench in the center. As he got closer he saw that it was a pew. A man and a woman were sitting upon it sleeping. They appeared to be a married couple. The wife's head was nestled on her husband's shoulder. Both were snoring loudly. He noticed that their feet were shackled to the pew.

"Hello!" he shouted at them, trying to arouse them, but there was no response from the sleeping pair. He shook the husband, but he remained sound asleep. Finally Pilgrim took one end of the pew and lifted it as high as he could, and then let it drop. The couple startled and stared at Pilgrim through groggy eyes.

"What are you doing here," Pilgrim asked.

"Just resting our eyes for a moment," the man replied.

"Who are you?"

"We are Church Members," they chimed in unison.

"What are you doing here?"

"We are worshipping in church, of course!" the man said indignantly. "We are always in church whenever the doors are open." Then they looked around in confusion. "At least we were in church listening to a sermon a moment ago.... It was a very informative sermon, too. Something about loyalty and faithfulness.... Anyway, the next thing we know, you are shaking us rudely."

"Well, you are not in church any more. You are in the middle of a field. It looks to me as if your church has crumbled to the ground ages ago. There is nothing to keep you here now. Come with me to the Celestial City."

"Oh no, we can't. We must remain faithful to our church. Our ancestors built this church, and we will be loyal to the end."

"Well, the end has come!" observed Pilgrim. "Look around you. Your church is long gone. Come with me. We can be a church together on the road. Our Lord said, 'Where two or three of you are gathered in my name....'"

"You can't have church on the road!" said the wife, with a toss of her nose. "Everyone knows a church is for sitting, not walking." Her husband nodded in agreement. Then in unison they yawned, closed their eyes and fell back asleep.

Pilgrim went on his way shaking his head, sad that church members preferred sitting and sleeping to the pilgrimage of faith.

TWO TRESPASSERS

As Pilgrim walked the lane, he saw the top of a ladder suddenly appear atop the hedgerow up ahead. Two figures hurriedly scrambled over it, jumping into the narrow Way. They waited for Seeker to catch up, and then introduced themselves. One was named Expedient and the other Pragmatic.

"Where did you come from, and where are you going?" asked Pilgrim.

"Like you, we are on our way to the Promised Land," they said together. "We are from the Land of Death and are seeking Life."

"How is it that you came over the hedge and not through the Gate?"

"Where we live everyone knows that the gate is too far, and the road is too steep. We discovered a shortcut that allows us to reach our destination in a fraction of the time that it takes others."

"But won't the Lord be upset with you?"

"Oh no! It does not matter HOW you get there. It just matters THAT you get there! As our father Practical used to say, 'The end justifies the means.'"

"But I do not see a mark on your foreheads and you are not wearing traveling clothes. Did you have your shame and guilt removed at the Cross? Did you receive new hearts?"

"Those are not necessary," said Pragmatic. "All that matters is that we believe the promise that our sins will be forgiven someday."

"As for the new heart," added Expedient, "it is overrated. Our hearts work perfectly fine, and they will see us to our destination. We can always trade them in for new ones in the future, if we need to."

"But you can receive a new heart now!" exclaimed Pilgrim, "All you have to do is go back the way you came, enter through the Gate and come to the Cross."

"Waste of time and effort!" they snorted together. "Why go backward when we can move forward? Aren't we now standing where you are? And with half the effort!"

"Yes, but the Lord told us to take the strait and narrow way. You will never make it to your destination by taking shortcuts."

"We will see who gets there first," replied Pragmatic. "I am confident that our way will take us to the end. See you in heaven! We'll save you a seat!"

With those words, the two grabbed the ladder and pulled it into the Way. They propped it against the hedge on the other side of the road and scrambled over. Pilgrim never saw them again.

SACRAMENT AND TRADITION

Pilgrim continued on his way. Shortly he saw ahead of him a couple of men dressed in liturgical vestments. Sweat dripped down their faces, and their shoulders drooped.

"Hello, there!"

"Greetings, brother," they responded.

As Pilgrim approached he saw the reason for their exhaustion. In addition to the heavy robes they wore, both were carrying enormous burdens. "My name is Pilgrim. May I inquire as to your names?"

"My name is Tradition," said one.

"I am Sacrament," said the other."

Sacrament had a large backpack. In the pack Pilgrim glimpsed loaves of bread, bottles of wine, containers of oil, and wedding jewelry, among other items. As if these were not enough to bring on the journey, he was also pulling a wagon which contained a baptistery and a confessional.

Tradition was similarly encumbered. He had liturgical stoles for every occasion, incense, candles, musical instruments, and a complete set of the Code of Canon Law. He also pulled a cart behind him, which contained a collection of statues depicting various saints, the largest of which was a life size image of the Mother of God.

Pilgrim grimaced in sympathy with the two men. "You look very tired. How long have you been on the Road?"

"Almost two thousand years now, and this is as far as we have gotten."

"How is it that you carry these things? You could not have brought them with you through the Gate."

"Oh, no. We were not allowed to bring anything through the Gate. We have accumulated these on our journey since then. Some of them we borrowed from the Theologian's house. Others we found along the way or crafted ourselves."

"Why do you carry them?"

"They are aids in our pilgrimage to the Promised Land."

"To be quite honest with you, they do not look like aids to me. They look like hindrances. I am very surprised that you did not rid yourself of them at the Cross."

At the mention of the Cross, Tradition's eyes brightened. "Just look at this. It is one of my most valued possessions." Tradition opened up one of his bags and rummaged through it. He removed vials of blood and pieces of bone and hair. It made Pilgrim nauseous to look at them. Finally he found what he was looking for. He withdrew a piece of wood about six inches long. "This is a piece of the true Cross, which we managed to remove from the base of the Old Rugged Cross. It used to be much bigger, but we have been taking off pieces for fellow pilgrims.

Would you like a piece? It will help you greatly on your journey!"

"No, thank you. The cross has already done its work in my life, and I do not need to carry a piece of it with me."

With a disappointed expression, Tradition put all the relics back into his bag.

"You are welcome to travel with me, if you would like," offered Pilgrim. "I could use the company. Sometimes this journey can be lonely."

"We would enjoy that very much."

So they continued the journey together. The going was much slower now. It was necessary for Pilgrim to stop frequently to allow his traveling companions to catch up. Furthermore they took rest breaks every few yards. But for the sake of fellowship Pilgrim walked with them for a mile or so, until they came to the foot of a hill called Difficulty.

The three stopped and assessed the way before them. The narrow path went straight up the hill, zigzagging up the slope. Pilgrim set out to ascend the hill when his companions called out. "Wait, we cannot climb that mountain with these loads!"

"It is not a mountain. It is only a hill, although I admit it is a steep one. Anyway we have no choice. The Way goes up the hill, and we must follow it."

"You can follow it if you wish, but we cannot."

"Why don't you leave your things here at the foot of the hill? You don't really need them, and I doubt very much if they will be of any use in the Promised Land."

"Oh, no! We cannot do that! Every one of these items is necessary to ensure that we reach our destination."

"They seem to be stopping you from reaching your destination!"

"That is easy for you to say! You are young and do not know how long and difficult this journey can be."

"What will you do now, if you cannot ascend the hill with all these items?"

"We will go around the difficulty, of course! We have been doing it all our lives."

Tradition and Sacrament pointed out to Pilgrim that two other roads went around the hill, one to the left and one to the right. Unlike the path up the hill, these roads were wide and smooth. "Perfect for cart-pulling!" observed

Tradition. "It is obvious that many pilgrims have traveled these roads. That is proof enough that it is a good way to travel. Let's go!"

Sacrament and Tradition loaded their burdens and went on their way – one to the east and one to the west.

"But what if these roads do not join the strait and narrow Way beyond the hill?" yelled Pilgrim after them. "We have faith that they will," Sacrament yelled back. "Faith in sacraments and traditions has got us this far, and we trust that it will bring us all the way."

And so they parted ways. Pilgrim heard later that Sacrament's road led into a dense forest from which there is no exit. Tradition's way went through a dark mountain valley where he stumbled and fell, unable to rise due to his load. His bones were discovered years later and were added to the reliquary that he had carried.

THE HILL OF DIFFICULTY

Pilgrim began climbing Difficulty Hill. At first he ran, to make up for lost time. But soon he was forced to slow to a walk. About halfway up the hill there was a shelter with a nearby spring. He rested there a while, meditating on the way he had come. Having been shaken by his experience with Sacrament and Tradition, he searched his heart for assurance that he was traveling the right route. His new heart spoke to him in a manner that his previous heart never had. He felt such assurance that all doubts dispersed. He drifted off into a peaceful sleep.

He was startled awake by the words, "Get up! Daylight is fading!" He looked around but saw no one. Pilgrim immediately continued his journey. When he reached the top of the hill, two women came running toward him. One was yelling, "Danger! Danger! Religious radicals!" The other said frantically, "There is a cult atop the hill. They will brainwash you and steal your money! Run for your life!"

The women would have hurried past him without explaining, but Pilgrim stopped them. "What are you taking about?"

"We climbed this hill, as you are now, and when we got to the top we saw two demons in human form," panted one of the women.

"They are guarding their temple of deception!" screeched the other. "We did not know they were demons until they spoke. Then it became clear to us. They are part of the Religious Right. They plan to take over our land and impose their social agenda on us! Run for your life! The End is near!" The women ran down the hill and out of sight.

Pilgrim took their warning seriously, but having come this far he was unwilling to turn back. He decided to continue his journey, confident that his new heart could discern truth from falsehood.

FIRST BAPTIST CHURCH

On top of the hill was a beautiful building. It was a large brick structure with a white steeple. A sign in front bore the words *First Baptist Church*. "Surely this is not the temple of doom that the women spoke of," mused Pilgrim. He decided to enter it, hoping someone could direct him to a place where he could spend the night. At the entrance to the church were two men with plastic name tags. One was identified as Bill and the other Check.

"Welcome, brother," they chimed together, giving him a hearty handshake and slap on the back. "It is good to have you at our service tonight. By the way, have you been saved?"

"Uh, I have come through the Gate, and my burden was lifted at the Cross."

"That is all very well," Bill responded. "But have you accepted Jesus Christ as your personal Lord and Savior?" Check added, "Have you been born again and baptized by immersion for the forgiveness of sins?"

"I was given a mark on my forehead, a new heart, and a new name."

"But are you in fellowship with a Bible-believing church? And more important, do you tithe your income as our Lord commands us?"

"I have no income at the present time," said Pilgrim.

Hearing those words, the two seemed to lose interest. But they continued to smile broadly, pressed a worship bulletin into his hand, and opened the church doors for him. He stepped into the lobby and was met with a blast of air-conditioning that took his breath away. The lobby was covered in wall-to-wall carpet. People were bustling around carrying copies of the Book.

He walked through another set of glass doors into the main sanctuary, where he saw row upon row of cushioned chairs. Music vibrated from speakers mounted on the walls of the auditorium. At the front of the sanctuary was a large glass pulpit. Pilgrim's first thought was how incongruous this interior was with the Hill of Difficulty located right outside the church doors.

Pilgrim took his seat. It felt good to rest his body, and he nearly fell asleep. Then the service began. A large choir sang beautiful songs. The music spoke of the Way, and it reassured Pilgrim that he was in the right place after all.

Then a man with a wide smile ascended to the pulpit. According to the bulletin this was Pastor Grin. His sermon was about reaching out to the community, expanding the ministry to a bigger campus, and the importance of giving money. There were a lot of numbers in the sermon: numbers of members, numbers of baptisms, numbers of children in Sunday School, numbers of youth in the Youth Program, numbers of people in worship. He talked about budgets, offerings, and deficits. It seemed that the Lord of this church was an Accountant who was very interested in figures. The preacher lifted up his copy of the Book and waved it a lot. He quoted the Book many times, but his message did not have much to do with the teachings that Pilgrim had read in the Book.

At the end of the worship service Pastor Grin gave what he called an "altar call." He invited people to come down the aisles to the front of the church to "receive Jesus as their personal Savior." Those who walked forward during the hymn would be saved, he assured them, although it was not clear to Pilgrim what they were being saved from or saved for. This salvation appeared to have very little to do with the journey to the Celestial City.

After the service people invited Pilgrim to attend the fellowship hour, where there would be refreshments. He was very hungry after his day's walk, so he accepted. Indeed there was a feast of donuts, pastries and coffee laid out on tables. He noticed for the first time that most of the members of this church were quite obese. "They don't do much walking," he thought.

After the fellowship hour, one attractive young woman asked if he would like to come to a Bible discussion that was meeting immediately in a nearby room. He accepted. The Bible Study was much more interesting than the Worship Service. These people had traveled the same journey he had made! They spoke about the Bog of Angst, the strait Gate and the narrow Way. With emotion in their voices they testified of the Old Rugged Cross and the dangers of the Way. The discussion went well into the night. After the Bible Study one nice couple named Fundy asked Pilgrim if he would like to spend the night at their house. He accepted their hospitality with gratitude.

The next morning he returned to First Baptist Church with the couple. There was something going on at the church every day of the week, they explained. You could spend your whole life at this church and never have to meet an unbeliever. It was such a safe and family-friendly place to be, they gushed.

At the church they insisted on showing him the Museum of Famous Baptists. A tour guide escorted them through the exhibit. First there was a statue of John the Baptist, clothed in what they said was a garment of real camel's hair. He was depicted as eating grasshoppers.

"I thought that Baptists began in the 17th century," wondered Pilgrim aloud.

"Oh, no. Baptists go back to the beginning – even before Jesus. Jesus was a Baptist because John the Baptist baptized him. By immersion ... of course! There is a Trail of Blood from them, throughout history right up to today. Baptists all the way down! The Lord has never left himself without a witness."

"Hmmmm. What about those grasshoppers. I read in a Bible commentary that the "locusts" that John ate were actually the beans of the locust tree. We call it carob today."

"The Book clearly says locusts, and everyone knows that locusts are grasshoppers. If the Book says it, we believe it! Don't you believe the Book?"

"Of course I do. But I was instructed at the Theologian's House to read the Book literately, not literally."

They gave Pilgrim a sour look, and then brought him to see some of the other exhibits in the museum. There was a copy of the Book that Billy Graham used at his first Crusade.

They showed him another book, which they claimed was the most read book ever written (apart from the Book, of course). It had a very long title: *The Pilgrim's Progress From This World to That Which Is to Come: Delivered under the Similitude of a Dream Wherein is Discovered, The Manner of His Setting Out, His Dangerous Journey; and Safe Arrival at the Desired Country.* Pilgrim thumbed through it. Even though it had been written nearly four centuries earlier, it paralleled the journey that he was taking very accurately. He did not have the time to read it now, but he vowed he would return someday and read it all.

Nearby was a replica of the statue in the Lincoln Memorial. "Abraham Lincoln was a Baptist? I didn't think he was religious."

"He was raised a Baptist," they whispered, "So we claim him as our own. Especially since he was the first Republican president."

There were many other Baptist memorabilia. There was the pulpit of one they called the Prince of Preachers.[7] There was a room dedicated to missionaries, including Adoniram Judson, Lottie Moon, and William Carey.

"Now we are going to bring you into the most important room." They pulled open a heavy door and – much to Pilgrim's surprise – ushered him into an armory. It was filled with every type of weapon you could imagine. A variety of automatic weapons hung on the walls. Handguns of all calibers were displayed in cases. There were bullet proof vests, military style helmets, grenades, barriers, riot shields, face shields, riot gloves, blockades, combat boots, and much more.

"What is this place?"

"It is the Armory of God."

"But I thought that the Armor of God was metaphorical."

"Oh, no. It is very real. And anything here is yours for the taking. Before you leave – if you decide to leave – we will outfit you with everything you need to survive the Way."

"What do you mean?"

"Anything you want is yours. You paid the price when you entered through the narrow Gate and knelt at the foot of the Cross. You don't think our Lord would let you travel this Road unprotected did you?"

"I did not realize that I needed physical weapons and body armor."

"Of course you do! The Way is not a pleasant stroll through the countryside. It is a military campaign. The spiritual life is a battlefield. The journey is war."

"Against whom would I use such weapons?"

"Zombies!"

"Zombies?"

"Of course. You don't think those are metaphorical too, do you?"

"Well, yes. I thought they were fantasy."

"Oh, no. They are very real. So are demons, witches, abortionists, evolutionists, and Democrats!"

They moved to a side room off the armory where there were shelves of books and gifts. The books were mostly treatises about how to defeat enemies, including Harry Potter enthusiasts. This disturbed Pilgrim, because he remembered what Theologian had told him about J.K. Rowling. There was a line of pink chastity belts for girls and DVDs on pure living for boys. One whole wall was filled with colorful tracts, which looked similar to the ones that Campus Crusader carried with him.

When Pilgrim walked out of the building he was in shock. These people had seemed so normal the day before, but now he was starting to think that the two women at the top of the Hill of Difficulty may have been right.

"There is something we have been wanting to say to you," the Fundys said. "We would like to invite you to stay here at First Baptist permanently."

"Permanently? How could I? I am on a journey to the Promised Land."

"Yes, we know. But the Way is very dangerous. The chances are you will not make it to the End. There are jihadists, terrorists and liberals everywhere. If you stay with us behind these church walls you would be safe. When you die - hopefully of old age - you will be instantly transported to the Promised Land. So why risk premature death?"

"I appreciate your concern, but I did not begin this journey just to stop at the first sign of difficulty. I really must continue."

"We thought you might say that. In that case, we insist that you are outfitted with the Whole Armor of God."

So they brought him back into the armory. They fitted him with body armor and a helmet with a face shield. They put shin guards on his legs. They put an ammunition belt around his waist and combat boots on his feet. They gave him a Colt AR-15 Carbine semi-automatic rifle with a pistol grip, telescopic stock, and flash suppressor. Into his breast pocket they placed a camouflage edition of the Book, with which to defeat all the plans of the evil one.

They said to him, "Be strong in the Lord and in the strength of his might. For we fight against flesh and blood, against the schemes of unbelievers in high places, and the powers of darkness in high office." With those words they sent Pilgrim on his way.

PART 4

IN THE VALLEY

Pilgrim followed the trail down the Hill of Difficulty. He had considered the climb up the hill to be challenging, but the descent was even worse. On the way up his heart had pounded and his lungs had strained due to the steepness of the ascent. Coming down was a different matter. His knees began to hurt unbearably because of the weight of the equipment he was carrying. Furthermore the path was slippery due to springs and rivulets that seeped from the rocks. He slipped and fell in several spots. When he finally made it to the bottom, he rested, and ate some of the field rations that the people at First Baptist Church had provided him. Then he continued on his way.

BATTLE WITH APOLLYON

In the valley at the foot of the hill he saw a giant creature coming across the field toward him. The stench of the foul creature preceded him. He looked like a monster out of one of Pilgrim's fantasy books. He had the appearance of a dinosaur, but this was no dinosaur Pilgrim had ever read about. His body was covered in armored scales, and his tail was like a Stegosaurus. He had wings like a Pterodactyl, legs like a Brontosaurus, and teeth like that a T-Rex. To complete the image of a storybook dragon, out of the creature's mouth came fire and smoke. His name was Apollyon.

Pilgrim's hands and legs involuntarily began to shake at the sight of the beast. He had barely recovered from the descent down the Hill, and had no strength to face this behemoth. He thought for a moment about retreating. But he reconsidered, "If I turn and run I will be more vulnerable than if I stood my ground. This enemy looks like a wild animal. If I run, it will surely chase me down and devour me. I have no choice but to stand my ground!"

Apollyon approached Pilgrim and looked at him with disdain. He spoke with a human voice. "Does the Tyrant of the Far Kingdom, think so little of me that he would send a boy against me? Who are you? Where did you come from, and where are you going?"

"I am Pilgrim. I come from the Shadowlands, and I am headed toward the Land of Light."

"Shadowlands? That is my kingdom! You are one of my subjects. Bow to me, and I will spare your life!"

"I used to be one of your subjects, but I live there no longer. Now I am a citizen of that Land to which I am headed."

"Not so fast! Once a citizen of mine, always a citizen. Do you have emigration papers?"

"I have no documents, but I have a new heart upon which is written the land of my rebirth. And I have a new name that identifies me as a citizen of that Pure Land."

"What is that name?"

"Only I and my Lord know."

"Nonsense! You are making it all up. You are an illegal alien. No one wants you or will take you. The Pure Land you speak of has a wall and a river separating it from here, and no one can enter. Turn around now, and I will not kill you."

"I will not return to that dark place."

"In that case prepare to enter an even darker place, a place of eternal torment where there is weeping and gnashing of teeth."

With those words Apollyon attacked. Pilgrim shouldered his assault rifle and pressed off a few rounds. The bullets bounced off the creature's armored plates as if they were pebbles. Apollyon swung his tail to take Pilgrim off his feet. Pilgrim barely managed to get out of the way in time.

Fire and brimstone roared from Apollyon's mouth like a flamethrower. Pilgrim managed to get his riot shield in place just in time.

Pilgrim realized that he was no match for this monster. For one thing he was not able to maneuver well in this body armor. His weapon was useless against the armored plates of the beast. Then he recalled a story from the Book. What did he have to lose?

He found temporary cover behind a boulder and quickly shed the armor and weapons, which the Baptists had given him. They might be effective against flesh and blood, but this creature was neither! He recounted the Bible story in his mind and looked for some round stones. He formed a makeshift sling from the strap of his rifle. Now he was set to take on this giant beast. A couple of well-flung stones into the beast's eyes would do the trick!

Then he came to his senses. What the hell was he thinking? A sling and a few stones against a giant supernatural dinosaur? Was he crazy? Think, Pilgrim! Are there such things as monsters? Is that rational? Of course not! It makes for an interesting children's story or a fantasy novel, but it is not real life. There are no such things as fire-breathing dragons or zombies or demons! Have you completely lost your mind? Use your head!

With a sigh of relief he came out from behind the boulder with his eyes wide open. There was no creature in sight. No foul scent filled the air. Only the fragrance of wildflowers filled the valley. Those Christians at First Baptist Church had filled his mind with fearful fantasies. There are no monsters under the bed, no boogeymen in the closet. And in the real world there are no devils stalking Christians. With a satisfied grin he shook the dust off his feet and continued his journey, leaving the armor and weapons where they lay.

The Valley of the Shadow of Death

The valley narrowed into a deep, dark canyon called the Valley of the Shadow of Death. The Way led straight through it. This gorge looked far more dangerous than any terrain that had come before. As soon as he began his descent into the ravine, two men came running out toward him. At first he thought they might be enemies, and he reached instinctively for his weapon, but remembered that he had none. Then he realized that they were pilgrims like him.

"What is the matter? Why are you running?" he asked.

They gesticulated wildly, "Go back! Go back!"

"Why? Is there another monster like Apollyon ahead? If so, he is no danger to me."

"No, it is a thousand times worse. The valley itself is the enemy. It has the power of death in it. It holds fear and dread that no man can master. If you value your life or your sanity, you will find a way around."

"There is no other way. The Way leads straight through this valley, and I will follow it no matter what."

The two men ran past him, and Pilgrim continued on his way, although more carefully than before. Though he no longer feared demons and monsters, he knew there were very real dangers in the world that could destroy him.

The valley turned into a steep gorge and then into a deep chasm. As the walls grew higher and steeper, the path grew darker and darker. At this point the trail wound along one craggy wall of the ravine. The right side of the trail dropped off steeply. It was so steep that he had to pay close attention to where he was placing his feet so as not to fall. It was so deep and dark that the valley beneath him appeared like a bottomless abyss.

As he walked, the Way grew darker until he was unable to see his feet or the path. He had to feel his way inch by inch with his hands along the cliff wall. Then the left side of the trail also dropped away, and he was walking atop a narrow ridge in total darkness. In this darkness he began to hear cries and screams from the left, as if countless people were in torment far below. It felt to him like the cries of the damned writhing in hell. He put his hands to his ears to block the sound, but it could not eliminate it completely. Besides he needed his arms to balance himself on the ridge trail.

In the darkness his imagination began to play tricks on him. In his mind's eye he envisioned damned souls thrashing in pain, suffering endless torment at the command of a fearsome God. He imagined himself among them. His fear began to get the better of him, and he nearly tottered off the path.

He paused to assess his situation. Here he was on a razor's edge in the darkest of valleys. On the right side was a bottomless pit of nothingness. He knew in his heart that if he fell into that abyss, he would die forever. He would cease to exist. The thought of nonexistence filled him with fear and dread.

If he fell into the other side of the path he would descend into hell, which was far worse.

There he would suffer eternally for his sins. Which was worse? To be in agony for all eternity or to permanently cease to exist? He was frozen in place on that narrow way, unable to move forward or backwards. He began to lose his sense of balance, and he knew that any moment could be his last.

Tottering on the edge of the ravine, he thought he heard a voice calling to him. He inched forward a little, and it seemed stronger. It said, "Yea, though I walk through the valley of the shadow of death, I will fear no evil."

"Who are you?" Pilgrim cried out. There was a response, but he could not make out the caller's name. He thought it sounded like the name Occam, but he knew no one by that name. The voice spoke again and said, "Take the simple way."

"What do you mean?" Pilgrim replied.

The voice returned, "When there are two possibilities, the simplest is the better."[8]

What two possibilities? Forward or backwards? Right or Left? None of those were good options! Perhaps it had to do with his perception of the fates that awaited him on either side. On the left there appeared to be the pit of hell. Was that assessment the simplest explanation for the voices of torment he was hearing? Was it more likely that an entrance to hell lay beneath him or that he was imagining those voices? Furthermore, did it make sense that an eternal hell of endless torment really existed? Many preachers he had heard insisted it was real, but there is no evidence for it.

Such a place was not consistent with Pilgrim's understanding of an all-powerful, all-loving, all-just Deity. Eternal punishment for temporal sins is unjust by any human standard. Surely God is more just than humans. Torture is the handiwork of evil men. No loving God would stoop so low.

Which was more likely? That an all-loving, compassionate God would create - or allow to exist - a place of endless suffering where sinners were tortured for all eternity for things they did on earth? Or that this hellish place is the product of depraved human minds, which attributed it to God? The simplest explanation is that hell is the invention of the human heart, not the Divine Mind.

How about the endless abyss on his right? If he fell into that darkness he knew he would not only die, but he would cease to exist. If there were no hell, then if he died in a fall he would either go to heaven or he would cease to be. Are either of those choices something to fear? Heaven was not to be feared. If it exists, from all accounts it is a place of endless bliss. (Though he had to admit that the most descriptions of heaven he had heard sounded rather boring.) In any case it was not to be feared. But how about the other alternative? Was nothingness something to fear? His initial reaction was "Yes." He did not like the thought of blinking out of existence utterly and completely. But was this unwelcome fate something to fear?

When he thought about it more deeply he realized that ceasing to exist was not bad. If he did not exist, he could not be afraid! There would be no one to do the fearing. If death was nonexistence, then death was nothing. Therefore it was nothing to fear. The more he thought about it, the more he realized that he could not experience death. As long as he lived he was not dead. When he was dead he would not experience anything, including death. Death was the ceasing of all experience. Then why be afraid? As the philosopher said, "If I am, then death is not. If death is, then I am not. Why should I fear that which can only exist when I do not?"[9] Before Pilgrim was born he did not exist for billions of years, and that did not bother him one bit.[10] Why would future nonexistence be any different?

With the realization that he need not fear death or hell, he heaved a sigh of relief. A burden, as great as that which was lifted at the Cross, fell from him, and he was free to walk the Valley with confidence. As he began to walk again, he detected a faint light ahead in the distance. He moved in that direction. Even though the Way was still dark and narrow, he walked it now without fear. With each step the Way grew lighter until he was beyond the valley and standing in bright morning sunlight.

In the daylight he looked back at the road he had just traversed. He could see that the path was truly narrow with ravines on either side. But he also saw that the drop-offs on either side of the path were neither dark nor bottomless. There was no mouth of hell or bottomless pit. In fact in the sunlight they both looked to be pleasant dales with green pastures and still waters. There were no pitiful creatures writhing in pain and crying in anguish, as he had feared. What he had heard were only the sounds of goats and sheep grazing on mountain grass. "How different the world appears when seen in the light," Pilgrim mused aloud to himself.

The Valley of Dry Bones

As he walked in the light, the valley opened into a broad plain. Scattered across the field were human bones. It looked like an ancient battlefield where the dead soldiers had been left where they fell, their skeletons bleaching in the sun. On a bluff overlooking the battlefield was a cave where two giants lived. One was Calvin and the other Arminius. They spent their days bickering like two old spinsters. When they weren't fighting with each other, they sang their siren's song together, enticing pilgrims to turn aside from the Way. They had been doing this for centuries. The skeletons of shipwrecked faith were on display in the Valley below.

Under the giants' tutelage travelers were taught the art of theological disputation and rhetoric. They squared off into warring camps, each accusing the other of not being True Pilgrims. They spent their lives in theological disputes, growing old and dying in that place without ever continuing their journey to the Promised Land.

As Pilgrim picked his way through the Valley of Dry Bones, he noticed an old man with a pointed beard sitting at the cave entrance watching him hungrily. He knew instantly who it was. Calvin yelled to him as he passed by, "TULIP! TULIP! Tiptoe through the TULIP and you will be saved!" Pilgrim looked around, but he saw no flowers of any kind in that barren place. Besides it was not the season for tulips. Still the ecclesiastic cried at the top of his lungs, "TULIP! TULIP!"

It was clear to Pilgrim that too much learning had driven this churchman mad. He did his best to ignore the giant. But when Pilgrim turned his back, the polemicist yelled all the more, "You are not one of the elect! Christ did not die for you! You will never persevere to the End. It is predestined. You are damned forever, and rightly so!" As Pilgrim walked out of earshot, he thought he heard another voice responding to the first, yelling, "Freedom! Freedom!" And he could swear he heard the rattle of bones.

Part 5

Religious

As Pilgrim walked along the path he came to a small rise in the road. From there he could view the road ahead, and he noticed another traveler on the way. "Wait up!" he yelled. Instead the figure hurried even faster. Pilgrim raced to catch up, but stumbled and fell just as he reached the man. The other pilgrim stopped to help. Pilgrim recognized him immediately as a neighbor from his hometown. He was known as Religious.

"Thanks for stopping to help," Pilgrim said. "But didn't you hear me call earlier?"

"Yes, I did, but I did not want to stop or slow down. I am in a hurry to reach my goal."

"But would it not be beneficial to have a friend with you along the way?"

"Yes, it would, but I did not think you considered me a friend."

"Why is that?"

"Because you did not think to invite me to come with you on this journey. When we were both in the Shadowlands I had hoped that we could travel this road together. But you were so caught up in your own plans that you never even thought to ask me to accompany you."

"I am very sorry for that, friend. It is true that I could think of nothing and no one but myself at that time. Otherwise I would have asked you to join me. Will you join me now?"

"I would be glad to." So they continued their journey together, discussing their adventures along the way.

Pilgrim inquired, "How long did you stay at home after I left?"

"I stayed until I could not stand it any longer."

"What do you mean?"

"After you left, all that the townspeople could talk about was you!"

Pilgrim was taken aback. "Really? Why?"

"Before you left, no one really noticed how dingy and dark it was in that town. People had gotten used to it. Once you pointed it out – and decided to escape – people began to panic. They called it Climate Change. They said that they remembered how it used to be sunnier, warmer and happier in the town. But gradually over the years things changed. They had not paid attention to the change until you pointed it out.

Now it is all people can think about. Most people came to the conclusion that unless something is done, the land will be uninhabitable. People are very scared."

"Did others leave when they realized the gravity of the situation?"

"That is the strange thing. They talked a lot about it, but no one did much of anything. Some people took to going outside only in the middle of the day to cut down on what they called their "shadow footprint." They held vigils and lit candles to call attention to the darkness. They had forums to discuss it. Some carried flashlights with them at all times to shine on their shadows. But no one felt any urgency to evacuate. Eventually I could wait no longer, and so I set out for the Land of Light."

"How about Tolerant? Did he make it back okay?" asked Pilgrim.

"Yes, he did. He told stories about traveling with you. He talked at length about the Bog of Existential Angst. How he escaped it, but you did not. He said that you died in that place. I am glad he was mistaken."

"Yes, he left me to die there, without even looking back or trying to help. But I do not hold it against him. I am glad he made it home. Is he doing well?"

"No, not at all. The smell of that swamp clings to him still. People have shunned him, and not only because of the stink. His previous friends criticize him for walking with you for as long as he did. They accuse him for being a closet Intolerant. Others criticized him for abandoning you at the bog. They said that was immoral and unethical. Others called him a coward for beginning the journey and then turning around. He is in a very bad way now. Some call him a dog who has returned to his vomit. In any case I think he will never leave that place again. I fear that the shadows will overtake him, and he will die there."

Sensual Pleasure

"That is really sad. Well, let's talk about something more edifying. Tell me about your encounters on the Way. I have met many interesting characters and learned much, and I am sure you have also. Tell me about them."

So Religious did. "I came to the same Bog that you did, but I did not fall in. Because of the warning that Tolerant had given, I looked carefully for a way across. I saw stepping stones that had been laid across that swampy ground and walked across without incident. I made it the rest of the way to the Gate without any problem.

"A short time after the Gate I met a woman named Sensual Pleasure. I confess that I spent several days – and nights – with her at her house. I was tempted to remain there at her home. Then I realized that there is more to life than the pleasures of the flesh. I asked her to come with me on my journey, but she would not hear of it. I had to choose. So I chose the Way."

LICENSE

"Did you meet anyone else on the Way?"

"Yes, at the bottom of the Hill of Difficulty I met a man named License. He tried to discourage me from climbing the hill. He insisted that hardship was completely unnecessary in the spiritual life. In fact he scolded me for leaving Sensual Pleasure behind. He said that was very unchivalrous of me. She was a nice lady, he said, whom he had known for many years, and she deserved better.

"He explained that the best way to live life was to follow the instincts of our bodies and the impulses of our desires. The Creator made us the way we are, and all impulses are holy. The way of the flesh was not at odds with the way of the spirit, he explained. In fact pleasure is a sure indication that we are on the right path. That is how he knew that ascending the Hill of Difficulty was a mistake. There are always alternative ways around difficulties. He repeatedly said: 'Why take the hard way when you can take the easy way?'"

"How did you respond to him?"

"I thought about his words. It certainly would be nice to live an easier life. But then I remembered what my father said. He said that it is better to face difficulty than to avoid it. So I thanked License for his opinion and climbed the hill instead."

Legalist

"Good for you! Did you see anyone else?"

"Halfway up the hill I came to a resting place which had a small shelter with a spring, which I drank from. I took a short nap there."

"Yes, I know the place! I stopped there, too."

"I was mugged at that spot by a man named Legalist. He began to beat me for taking a rest, saying repeatedly, 'There is no rest for the weary!' He called me all sorts of names, even accusing me of being a follower of License. I assured him I was not, but he did not believe me. He said that my actions spoke louder than words. The fact that I was resting meant that I was a sluggard."

"Who was the mugger?"

"He did not tell me his name. But let me tell you what happened. He kept hitting me with his fists and kicking me. I asked him why he was doing this. He said it was because I was a sinner and that all the inclinations of my heart were sinful all the time. He repeatedly quoted the verses, "For all have sinned and fallen short of the glory of God" and "None are righteous, no not one." He beat me into unconsciousness. When I woke up I cried for mercy, but he said there was no mercy for the wicked. I was sure that I was going to die in that place, but then someone told him to stop."

"Who said it?"

"I didn't know at first. But then I saw the scars in his hands and feet, and I knew it was the Lord."

"I think I know the name of the man who beat you. He is Legalist. He believes that the only way to live is to obey the Law of God precisely. He considers himself to be a great interpreter and enforcer of the Book. He knows no mercy. It is only by the grace of God that you escaped from him."

"Amen to that!"

"Did you make it to the top of the hill?"

"Yes, I did."

"And did you go into First Baptist Church?"

"No. I saw the building, but the two men outside were dressed exactly like my assailant. I was afraid they were his friends and would attack me. When they saw me coming they began to come toward me. That scared me so much that I ran past the church and immediately continued down the hill."

"That must have been when you passed me. I wish you would have stopped. They would have shown you some amazing things. I am still pondering them now. Furthermore we could have traveled together from that spot on. I could have used your help at the bottom of the hill! By the way did you meet anyone in the valley below the hill?"

BORED

"I met a man name Bored, who was traveling in the opposite direction. He had the most disagreeable expression on his face. He told me that the Way was not at all what he expected. He imagined that it would be inspiring and uplifting, filled with inspirational music and edifying sermons. But so far it had been nothing like that. He said he was on his way home to the Shadowlands where he had a good church. I asked why he had left that church in the first place. He replied that it had become old and stale. The preacher did not preach the whole gospel, and the other church members were not very spiritual. That is why he had set out on the journey. But now he realized that the Way was even less interesting, so he was returning home."

"What did you say to him?"

"I told him that the Way was not meant to cater to our religious tastes. I said he needed to persevere to the end. But he was not interested."

"Did you meet anyone else?"

Judgmental

"Yes, I encountered a woman named Judgmental. She was the most disagreeable person I have ever met. She said she had traveled with Bored for a while, but he was not spiritual enough. At first Judgmental appeared to me to be a pilgrim, but the more I spoke with her, the less I held that position. Everything that came out of her mouth was negative. She did not have a good word to say about anyone or anything."

"Can you give me some examples?"

"Lots of them! She said that the food on the Way was not up to her standards. She was a vegetarian, and all they served at the inns was meat! Furthermore it was red meat, something she would never touch.

"She went on and on complaining about her husband. His name is Faithful, but she said he did not live up to his name. All he did was work, work, work. He never spent any time with her. He was always doing things the wrong way. He was always forgetting things. He never took her feelings into consideration when it came to decisions. He was very inconsiderate, according to her."

"Where was her husband? Why were they not traveling together?"

"She said that he had gone on ahead. That was just like him, she complained. He was always in a hurry. She said that he had been wanting to come on this journey for years, but she had more important things to do with her life. Finally he gave her a deadline. If she was not ready by the next morning, he was leaving without her. Well, it turns out that she did not sleep well that night. There were interesting things to watch on TV and magazines to read. She was still in bed when the hour came to leave, so he left without her. She left a few hours later – so she said - and has been trying to catch up to him ever since. But he will not answer his cell phone, though she calls him twenty times a day."

"Poor man! Why did Faithful ever marry her?"

"Apparently he loves her deeply, but he loves the Lord more. That is why he left for the Celestial City."

"What else was she critical about?"

"What was she NOT critical about!? She was critical about every church but her own, everyone's theology but her own, every political position but her own. Meeting her was the most disagreeable experience I have ever had. It took me days to recover from the encounter and get her voice out of my head! I don't know how Faithful stood it for so long. I hope for Faithful's sake that she never catches up with him. Actually I do not think she will. She was walking very slowly, mumbling constantly about the roughness of the road, the dampness in the air, and the brightness of the sun. Whew! What a mess! I was never as glad as when I left her behind."

"Did you meet anyone else in the Valley after her?"

"No, I did not. It was a quiet trip for me through the rest of the valley and even through the Valley of the Shadow of Death."

"Really?" explained Pilgrim. "You did not find that hard going?"

"Not at all. It was sunshine all the way."

"How about Apollyon?"

"You mean the devil? I heard about him, but never caught sight of him."

"I had just the opposite experience. I had to battle Apollyon and barely made it through the Valley of the Shadow of Death alive."

SPIRITUAL BUT NOT RELIGIOUS

As they traveled along the Way, the road became noticeably wider. Religious noticed a woman walking to one side. She was a tall, attractive woman, dressed in stylish hiking clothes. Religious called out, "Sister, are you traveling to the Beautiful Country?"

"Yes," she replied.

"Great! We are headed there also. Would you like to walk with us?"

"That would he wonderful! I was getting kind of lonely traveling by myself."

So they walked together.

"My name is Religious, and this is my friend Pilgrim. May I ask your name?"

"My name is Spiritual But Not Religious."

"That is a very interesting name. But to be honest it sound like an oxymoron. How can one be spiritual but not religious? Doesn't one necessarily entail the other?"

"Oh, no. Just the opposite. In fact the more religious one is the less spiritual – and vice versa."

A flush of annoyance come from deep inside within Religious and spread over his face, but he tried to contain it. "Would you please explain that," he said. "You see I am religious, and I consider myself also a spiritually-minded person."

"I congratulate you on that feat. But I have found that religion stunts spiritual growth. Let me tell you a little about myself and perhaps you will understand better."

"By all means! It is a long journey, and I would enjoy hearing about your life."

"I was born into a very religious family," Spiritual began. "They went to Sunday School and church every Sunday. When it came time to profess my faith and join the church, I did so enthusiastically."

"Praise the Lord!" interjected Religious.

"But when I went away to college I began to question the things I had been taught. I took philosophy, history, and religion classes. I learned things they never taught me in church. I began to explore other religions as well. I read the Upanishads and the Bhagavad Gita. I studied the Sutras and the Quran. I read the Tao Te Ching and the Analects. I learned that there are many beautiful spiritual paths in the world. Furthermore they are just as moral and spiritual as the faith I was raised in.

"In time I came to understand that there are many roads to the Common Destination that we call the Celestial City. It does not really matter what one believes. It does not matter what gods we worship. They are all faces of the One True God. As long as we believe in Spiritual Truth and sincerely seek to live by its light, then we are on the right path. All religions are different paths up the same spiritual mountain."

"That is a very interesting perspective," said Pilgrim, who had been silently listening to the conversation between his two companions. "But I learned some other things at the Theologian's House. Did you, by any chance, stop there on your way?"

"I met the man outside his house, and he invited me in. But I had already studied theology in college, so I did not enter."

"That is too bad. In his house I learned that there are many ways of looking at things, but nearly all of them are wrong. Rather than all paths being equally good and true – as you suggest – I saw that most people are blind to the bigger picture. People are like the proverbial blind men who mistake a part of the elephant for the whole."

"Exactly!" said Spiritual. "I see the whole!"

"I don't think so. You see superficial similarities between religions and conclude they are all essentially the same. They are not. They are not all paths up the same mountain."

"I can see now that you are not spiritual at all. You sound just like the religious hypocrites in the church I grew up in. I do not think we can walk together any longer!" Then she abruptly stepped off the path.

Pilgrim called after her, "But I thought you said that all paths lead to the same destination. So why can't you walk with us on the Way a bit longer, since we are going to the same place?"

"Your Way is true for you, but not for me. You are far too unspiritual for me to tolerate your company any longer. I prefer to go take a more enlightened road. Namaste!"

With those parting words, Spiritual But Not Religious immediately took a side path into a dark wood. It did not look safe to Religious, who called after her and urged her to return. But she began to chant a mantra very loudly and walked on.

PART 6
MEGACHURCH

They were almost out of the countryside and coming close to civilization when Religious happened to glance back at the way they had come. In the distance he noticed a figure walking behind them. They decided to wait for him. When the person got closer Religious recognized him. "It is my old friend Billy Graham!" he exclaimed.

"Billy Graham? You know the great evangelist?" asked Pilgrim.

"Yes, he is the one who set me on the Path that we are now walking."

They waited for Dr. Graham to catch up to them. As soon as he was close, Billy Graham recognized Religious, and greeted him warmly.

"This is my friend Pilgrim," Religious said.

"I have heard of you," responded Billy. "My friend Campus Crusader told me that you had embarked on the way to the Other World."

"You know Campus Crusader?"

"Yes, indeed. We have similar ministries. Although my calling has been to preach to multitudes and his has been to reach individuals. But it is the same message."

"It is an honor to meet you," said Pilgrim. "I have watched your crusades on television and read some of your books. I especially enjoyed the one about heaven and eternal life."

"Thank you very much. Religious, tell me about your journey since we last met. You, too, Pilgrim. The stories of all believers are interesting to me, even when I am not the one who guided them to the Gate."

So Religious and Pilgrim told Reverend Graham of their adventures on the Way. They described for him the difficulties and temptations they had faced, their failures, and their recoveries.

"I am glad. Not because you have faced trials and temptations, but because you have overcome them and are still on the Path. The seed that I and my fellow evangelist sowed has taken root. You have persevered to this point."

Religious thanked Reverend Graham for his encouragement, and asked if he could give them some advice concerning the road ahead. Pilgrim echoed that request by nodding his head vigorously.

"My sons, through many dangers, toils and snares you have already come. But I warn you that the worst is yet to come. You have been traveling through the wilderness, which has its unique types of dangers. Soon you will come to a city, which poses worse dangers. It is filled with people who have stopped traveling the Way.

"No one is more dangerous than a believer who has stopped short of the Goal. He – or she – has much guilt and shame because he has resisted the Spirit by refusing to travel further. They resent those who desire to go further. They will hesitate at nothing to stop a seeker from seeking for more than they have. Their shame and fear swell into anger and hate. You have not encountered such people yet, but you will shortly."

"Will we survive their attacks?"

"I am not a prophet. But I have seen enough of life to have a reliable instinct about spiritual dangers. I suspect that one – if not both – of you will die for your faith. I believe that is why the Lord has arranged our meeting here today at the outskirts of the city ahead – to give you strength and hope. Do not be afraid! Be faithful unto death, and you will receive the Crown of Life. Be assured that if you die while faithfully walking the Way, you will be immediately ushered into the Presence of our Lord. That one will avoid the hardships of the rest of the journey, which the one who survives must endure. When you come into the city, remember my words. Be of good courage."

With those words Billy Graham departed.

Prosperity Gospel Ministries

Pilgrim and Religious emerged out of the wilderness and approached the outskirts of a city named Megachurch. In that city there was a popular church called Prosperity Gospel Ministries. The name sounded modern and the building was new, but the movement traces its roots back thousands of years. Its leaders say that it goes back to Abraham and even before that to Job. As long as there have been pilgrims traveling on the Way, there has been the Prosperity Gospel. The advocates of these ministries saw themselves as "equipping the saints for ministry" by providing them with material wealth and psychological well-being.

The building that housed the Prosperity Gospel Ministries looked like a huge shopping mall or sports arena. Outside the building were huge signs bearing the image of the senior pastor. He was a middle aged man with curly black hair and a bright white smile that reminded Pilgrim of the grin worn by the pastor of First Baptist Church. Beside the pastor stood his wife, a blond beauty bearing equally impressive bleached incisors. Pilgrim wondered if cosmetic dentistry was a requirement for being a religious leader in this land.

Pilgrim and Religious walked through one of the many entrances into the building. They were immediately engulfed by a cacophony of sounds and smells. It felt more like a huge shopping mall than any church that they had ever seen. There were shops around the edges of the space, and kiosks peppered the open area. Every imaginable product and service was being sold. There was Stars-in-Your-Crown coffee being served with Angelic Anise scones. Ice Cream shops sold flavors like Heavenly Hash, Chocolate Infinity and Carnal Caramel.

There were bookstores with shelves displaying books by the Smiling Pastor. There were DVDs and audio recordings of his messages. Titles included "How to Inherit the Wealth of Abraham," "Jesus Wants You to be Rich," and "You CAN Take It With You!" Study editions of the Book were filled with helpful annotations and articles. There were racks of T-shirts bearing the logo of the ministry. One shirt bore the name Vanity Fair, which the sales clerk explained was the name of Megachurch in olden times.

As they traveled through the large arena, they saw booths playing patriotic music and selling American Flags. Kiosks sold every imaginable form of apparel bearing the Stars and Stripes, from undergarments to eyewear. On the lower shelf of one display Pilgrim noticed sweatshirts and tees with the Stars & Bars.

Moving on, they saw trinkets and souvenirs. They noticed a Real Estate office selling Christian timeshares and retirement homes in "believer-only" communities. There were Christian bands playing music at either end of the mall. There were booths promoting Christian camps, Christian high schools, Christian colleges and Christian pre-schools.

There was a store promoting a Christian exercise video. On the stage was a trio of scantily clad young women doing aerobics to the beat of the latest contemporary Christian music. Religious noticed that a large crowd of young men gathered at that booth. Courses in Real Estate Flipping were promoted, as well as Stock Market investing. "The Lord knows where the market is headed, and you can too," the barker called out to bystanders. There were Christian dating services and Christian theatre troupes.

One crowded booth featured a video of a woman translating a sermon into sign language. Dozens of men and women were availing themselves of the free lesson, imitating the instructor. But there did not appear to be any hearing-impaired persons present. One store displayed gold crosses in large glass cases. Another looked like a gun show with hundreds of handguns and automatic weapons for sale. A sign informed the buyer that a cross or your favorite scripture verse could be engraved on the stock for an additional charge.

Nearby there were recruiting offices for all branches of the military. Politicians worked the crowd shaking hands and cuddling toddlers. The travelers overheard them talk about the need for prayer in schools, outlawing abortion, and teaching Intelligent Design in the classroom. Pilgrim and Religious continued walking through the church mall in a state of shock. Never before had they seen so many religious people who were so enthralled with the things of the world. They did not know what to do or think.

Finally Religious snapped. When he saw a booth selling pointed white hoods and robes embroidered with the name of his Lord, he lost his cool. Roaring loudly he overturned the table. He went to an adjacent booth selling Confederate flags, and he overturned those tables as well. To make matters worse he proceeded to kick over a kiosk selling copies of "The Myth of the Separation of Church and State" and editions of the Book with a White Supremacist logo on the cover.

Religious shouted, "My Father's House shall be called a house of prayer, but you have made it a den of hate!" Pilgrim grabbed Religious by the arm and tried to escort him out of the building quickly, but it was too late. Shopkeepers from the neighboring booths, sensing a threat to their businesses, tackled Religious and tied his hands behind him. All Pilgrim could do was follow the crowd as they dragged his friend toward Security.

On the way they mocked him. "Do you see anything you would like to buy? How about this nice noose?" "I buy the Truth!" he retorted. "What is Truth?" they responded. "You have been brainwashed by the media and fake news!" People mocked him as they traveled the length of the mall. Others kicked him and punched him as he passed by. Some called for his death. Meanwhile Pilgrim was swept up in the current of the crowd, trying to keep his eyes on his friend.

Finally the crowd made it to the Prosperity Gospel Ministries security office. The head of security took him into an interrogation room, while the mob waited outside. Meanwhile Pilgrim tried to keep a low profile. The proprietor of one of the shops saw Pilgrim and said, "You are this fellow's friend, aren't you?"

"No, not me. You must have me mistaken for someone else."

"I am sure I saw you in my bookstore together," said another.

"No, it must have been someone who looked like me."

"I served you food," said the barista from Crispy Cross Donuts. "You were both sitting at a table together."

"You are wrong! A curse on that heretic! I do not know him!"

The ferocity of Pilgrim's denial convinced his accusers, and they backed off.

Meanwhile Religious was in the room being interrogated. They asked him where he was from and where he was heading. They asked what he was doing at Prosperity Gospel Ministries wearing such worn and dirty clothing. "You obviously are not a follower of the Way," they observed. "Otherwise the Lord would have blessed you with better clothing."

Religious responded, "My Lord is a friend of the poor and needy. He has no place to lay his head." "Definitely not one of ours," one of the security officers snorted. They asked why he overturned the tables of the merchants. He replied, "Zeal for my Father's house consumed me."

"So you admit doing it?" they asked.

"It is as you say."

"What more proof do we need? He is obviously an enemy of the gospel."

"String him up!" shouted another.

From a back room they brought out a cage big enough to hold a man. They pushed Religious into it and posted a sign on it which read "Heretic and Traitor." They proceeded to carry the cage to the center of the mall, where they attached it to a cable hanging from the ceiling and hoisted it to head level. The security forces departed and left him to the mercy of the crowd. Only one officer remained to ensure they did not kill him.

Religious crouched in the cage for hours while people mocked and reviled him as they walked by. They spit on him. They threw garbage and trash at him through the bars. But Religious did not return evil for evil. Like his

Lord he quietly prayed, "Father, forgive them, for they know not what they do." All the while Pilgrim kept a lookout from some distance away, trying to look as inconspicuous as possible.

After several hours of being on display, the security guards returned. They lowered the cage, took Religious by the arms and brought him before the elders of Prosperity Gospel Ministries to be put on trial. The judge was none other than the pastor of the church. His name, Religious learned, was Media.

The indictment against the defendant was read. Judge Media spoke. "It has come to my attention that the defendant is an enemy combatant and therefore not entitled to a trial under the laws of God. But out of mercy and compassion the court will grant him a chance to defend himself. These are the charges brought against the defendant: That he is an enemy of the State and of our Lord, a disturber of the peace, a purveyor of 'fake news,' which he falsely calls 'good news.' He is a disturber of the peace and of fair trade. He has destroyed property and besmirched the reputation of our church and family values."

He turned to Religious and asked, "How do you plead?"

Religious responded, "I oppose only those who are opposed to my Lord and his Kingdom. I admit to overturning tables. That was done in a moment of passion. I will gladly repay the vendors for any loss they have suffered. Beyond that I admit no wrongdoing. I have harmed no one. I will not take back my words. I must speak the Truth. The truth is that you have turned the house of God into a marketplace. You have rejected the Law of God and followed human desires. You have replaced the Love of God with slogans of hate. I condemn this ministry, which you falsely call a church. This place is no house of God. It is an abomination in the sight of the Lord!"

The place erupted in shouts. "You have heard him yourself, what more evidence do we need," shouted the prosecutor. "Order! Order" commanded the judge. "We will continue with the trial. The prosecution will call its witnesses." Three witnesses testified. They were named Capitalism, Nationalism and Racism.

Capitalism spoke first. "I know of the defendant from when I lived in the Shadowlands, before I was baptized into the way of Christian Prosperity. I also heard him speaking to the crowd as he hung in the cage in our mall. I heard him say that our Lord was poor and had no place to lay his head. I heard him proclaim,

'Blessed are the poor' and 'Woe to you who are rich' and 'Sell all that you have and give to the poor and you shall have treasures in heaven.' He said these were the teachings of our Lord. But as we all know, these words have been taken out of context and do not mean that they appear to mean. In fact they mean the opposite." The courtroom erupted in cheers. "It is clear to me that the defendant is opposed to our way of life. He would have us feed our enemies and thereby cause the good people of our church to starve. For the good of our economy, he must die!"

Nationalism was next to take the stand. "I also have known the defendant from my time in the Shadowlands, before I came to see the advantage of combining church and state. I heard him say that the Ten Commandments should not be displayed on public property. I also heard him say that there should not be mandatory prayer in schools. He even advocates that the name of God be taken out of our Pledge of Allegiance!"

Shouts of "Traitor!" and "Atheist" filled the room.

Finally Racism was sworn in. "I was shopping at the business of my good friend Klansman when the defendant committed his crimes. I was an eyewitness to what he said and did today. He was envious of the quality merchandise that was being sold and purposefully destroyed it. He spoke words that are so detestable that they cannot be repeatedly in court. But for the sake of our Aryan heritage I must say them.

"He said that people of all races and colors are created equal. He said that the curse of Ham, which is taught in our holy Book, is a lie. He condemns slavery, which is clearly endorsed by Book. He said it was wrong for Joshua to exterminate the Canaanites and that King Saul should not have tried to kill all the Amalekites, even though it was the direct command of God. He defended the Christ-killers, and even suggested that our Lord was of their race. In short, the defendant is an enemy of our God, our Country, and our blessed Economy. If he is allowed to live, then your Honor will be complicit in undermining everything that we stand for!"

Everyone in the courtroom rose to their feet. People stomped their feet and pounded their fists, calling for an immediate end to the trial and the execution of this dangerous subversive. Finally Judge Media got control of the courtroom. "Are there any other witnesses?"

The prosecution said, "There are more that I could call. I was going to call Sexism and Homophobia to the stand. But I do not want to elongate this trial. The prosecution rests."

"Does the defense have any witnesses?" He asked.

Religious looked around the courtroom. He saw Pilgrim standing in the back with his eyes cast down, trying to hide in the crowd. "No, your honor" replied Religious. "But in my own defense I will say that I stand by my words. I am no traitor or heretic. I am a faithful follower of my Lord and Savior. And I look forward to meeting my Lord in heaven this day." Then Religious' face turned upward and seemed to glow with a heavenly light. "I see my Lord sitting at the right hand of God!"

"What more evidence do we need," declared the judge. "I declare the defendant guilty as charged. Take him outside the Ministry walls and execute him!"

The crowd carried Religious outside the gates. They whipped him and beat him into unconsciousness. They stoned him until there was only a piles of rocks where Religious had fallen.

Suddenly a chariot of fire pulled by two heavenly horses appeared in the sky and descended to the spot where Religious died. The rabble backed off in shock. The soul of Religious emerged from the pile of stones and climbed aboard the chariot. He was immediately taken into heaven as a trumpet sounded. When Judge Media heard about the ascension, he declared that it had never happened. "Fake news! The fact is that we let this man known as Religious leave peacefully. Let all news outlets proclaim the truth. "

As for Pilgrim, when the crowd dispersed he was left standing alone. He went off by himself and wept bitterly.

TRUTHFUL

Pilgrim left Prosperity Gospel Ministries that very day, and walked through the rest of the City of Megachurch. A man called out from behind him, "Wait up!" Pilgrim turned and recognized a man who had been in the crowd when Religious was stoned. "If you have come to take me back to Prosperity Gospel to be tried, I will not resist you. I feel bad enough that I did not stand up for my friend. I am at your mercy."

"Oh, no. I recognize you as a companion of Religious, but I have not come to arrest you. I have come to join you on your journey. The words and spirit of Religious touched me deeply. I want what he has. If you know where to find it, please let me travel with you."

"I am glad to have a companion. I am already lonely without Religious. I will never forget him, and I will never forgive myself for not coming to his defense."

"There was nothing you could have done. If you had spoken up, your bones would be laying with his under that pile of stones back there."

"That may be true. But it is also true that my spirit would be in the Land of Light now. Instead I walk this Way with guilt on my shoulders and sadness in my heart."

"It is true that you denied your friend. I heard you say three time that you did not know him. But remember the Disciple of our Lord, who denied him three times, yet went on to serve him faithfully. You can repent and start anew."

"Help me, please."

Pilgrim's new friend took him by the hand and they knelt together on the side of that road. Pilgrim wept and confessed that he had been unfaithful to his friend and to the Way. When he arose the burden of guilt had lifted from him. There was also the resolve that if ever he should find himself in the same type of situation that he would die rather than deny the Truth.

"I do not even know your name, though you have already proven to be more of a friend to me than I was to Religious."

"My name is Truthful."

Glassminster Cathedral

As they walked on together through the city, they passed church after church. Each one had billboards in front declaring them to be the most relevant, most friendly, and most welcoming church in the city. They were open twenty hour hours a day and provided everything from daycare centers and yoga classes to nail salons.

One building stood out from the others. It was a tall cathedral made entirely of glass. Etched across the front was its name: Glassminster. A man in a beautiful pulpit robe was standing on the steps of the building with his hands outstretched and a broad smile on his face.

He was reciting pithy sayings to passersby. "Tough times never last, but tough people do. Problems are not stop signs, they are guidelines. Turn your scars into stars."[11]

The travelers stopped to listen. "Those are interesting ideas."

"Thank you. You two look like you could use a little emotional pick-me-up. Come in and be refreshed. There is more of these inspirational thoughts inside."

"Do not take this the wrong way," replied Pilgrim, "but the last time we entered a church it resulted in the death of my friend."

"Oh, no. Nothing that negative would ever happen here. We are a purely positive congregation. My mission is to affirm you so that you can be all that you can be."

"May I ask your name?"

"Of course. I am the Reverend Doctor Self-Esteem, and this is my church," stretching his arms and beaming proudly. "I began preaching in a drive-in theatre, and now look at it my church. It was designed by one of the most famous architects in the land and financed entirely by people who wanted it to be all that it could be."

"To be honest, it looks a little fragile," said Truthful. "A rightly aimed stone could bring it all down."

"That is negative thinking. We can cure you of that. Just come in and listen to some of my prerecorded sermons. Or read some of my books - available for a small donation. Soon the cloud of negative thinking will disperse, and you will see clearly once again."

"Negative thinking is the problem?"

"Yes, and low self-esteem. The church today is in need of a New Reformation – the Self-Esteem Reformation! The problem is that we do not think enough of ourselves. We are always putting ourselves down. I will teach you to pull yourselves up!"

Pilgrim looked at him askance. "Our Lord taught us to deny ourselves. I always thought that self-centeredness – pride - was the problem, not the solution."

"Oh, no, no, no! That type of backward thinking is the problem. We need to think MORE of ourselves, not less. Our Lord said, 'Love your neighbor as yourself.' We can't love our neighbor unless we love ourselves first ... and best."

"That sounds like muddy thinking – not clear thinking - to me. I think I will stick with self-denial."

"You are not thinking clearly, friend. If you listen to your fears, you will die never knowing what a great person you might have been."[12]

"I think I see pretty clearly right now. I am seeing that this is not a place I want to enter. Goodbye."

With that they moved down the street. As they walked away they could hear him calling after them, "Let your hopes, not your hurts, shape your future."[13]

Pilgrim paused. "Actually, that sounds pretty good."

Truthful grimaced. "Don't even think about it!"

CHRISTIAN ENTERTAINMENT CENTER

They had not gone far beyond Glassminster Cathedral when they heard loud music emanating from speakers perched upon a building on the right side of the street. It looked like a conference center, but the digital signs out front declared that a Christian worship service was about to begin.

Pilgrim sighed. "I could use some time to worship our Lord. Let's give it a chance. We can sit in the back, and if it looks dangerous we can always slip out." Truthful acquiesced.

They entered the revolving doors. A crowd of people dressed in all sorts of clothing were milling around. The smell of popcorn was in the air. Candy and soft drinks were available at glass counters. CDs and T-shirts bearing the names of Christian bands were available for sale at booths.

Truthful grimaced. "Reminds me too much of the Prosperity Gospel. I think we should leave."

Pilgrim shook his head. "Let's give it a try. I really need to worship the Lord, even if it is not perfect."

They followed the crowds through another set of doors and into a huge auditorium with three levels of seating. The floors were carpeted, and the seats were cushioned. The lighting was dim, except for the spotlights on the stage where a band was warming up.

"This looks more like a concert than a worship service."

"As I said, let's give it a try."

People flowed in and filled the seats. The band started to play. Screens situated around the auditorium lit up with images. The band leader shouted. "Praise the Lord! Are you glad to be here?" The crowd cheered in response. Everyone rose to their feet, their hands in the air. Lyrics filled the screens, and the music began.

Truthful and Pilgrim were caught up in the moment. They whooped and cheered. They sang with the band. The beat was infectious, and the lyrics spoke of the goodness of the Lord. They smiled at each other. Yes, they were in the right place. After all they had been through, this was exactly what they needed - a place to forget their troubles and get caught up in the adoration of the Father and his Son.

The music went on and on. The same lyrics were repeated over and over. Truthful began to have doubts. "This might be a Seven Eleven church."

"Seven Eleven? You mean like the convenience store?"

"No, songs with seven words repeated eleven times. But this feels more like eleven hundred times. Look at the faces of the people."

Pilgrim looked around him. People seemed to be in a trance. Their hands were raised like toddlers reaching for a parent. Some faces wore blank expressions. Others were grimacing like they were in pain. Some had tears streaming down their faces.

"This doesn't feel right."

The music faded, leaving the audience in a state of receptivity. People waited in expectation.

A light went on in Truthful's head. "Mind control! This music is the same as a chant or a mantra. It is designed to induce an altered state of consciousness."

A man appeared on the stage. His name appeared on all the screens simultaneously: Pastor Showtime. He shouted, "God is fun…"

The congregation responded. "All the time!"

"And all the time…

"God is fun!"

Pilgrim was already running down the aisle toward the rear of the building. "Let's get out of here!" Truthful was on his heels. They reached the doors just as another song began.

"That was close!"

"That was not worship at all, was it?"

"No, it wasn't. It gave the impression of worship, but that was not the Spirit at work. That was psychological manipulation, pure and simple."

"Are there no real churches along the Way where we can be refreshed?"

THE MARKET-DRIVEN CHURCH

They trudged dejectedly down the city streets, passing storefront chapels and strip mall fellowships, all trying to imitate the megachurches. Many churches advertised a program called "Forty Days of Marketing." One particularly large church with an orange grove in the front yard had a sign that identified it as the Market-Driven Church. An obese man in a Hawaiian shirt was standing at the front door waving for them to come in.

"What does that mean? Market-driven?" Pilgrim asked his friend.

Truthful's face distorted into an expression of disgust. "It means that they will sell whatever the Christian market wants. Their motto is 'Whatever works.' It is sometimes called Consumer Christianity or Designer Christianity. It is very popular and very successful. The pastor that you see in the Hawaiian shirt is named Pragmatist. He is famous and is even on the President's Council of Religious Advisers. This church is more dangerous than the others because its message can sound like the gospel of our Lord. But do not be deceived. It has nothing to do with the Strait and Narrow Way. It follows the Way of Least Resistance."

The Miracle Tabernacle

They walked until twilight, avoiding several obviously fraudulent churches, such as the Dianetics Discovery Center and the Moroni Meetinghouse. On the outskirts of Megachurch the travelers approached what looked like a traveling circus. In the dusk of the setting sun, the lights shone with a supernatural brilliance. A carnival barker was at the gate, exhorting passers-by to step up and view "the miraculous power of God to heal."

"Do you have one leg shorter than the other? Are you the victim of migraines? God does not want you to be sick. The Lord can heal you tonight! Just step right into the Miracle Tabernacle. Evangelist Ben Hinny has demonstrated the Lord's power to heal physical, spiritual and emotional ailments, just as the Lord promises in his Word."

"The Book does speak about giving believers the power to heal," Pilgrim wondered aloud. "Do you think this could possibly be the real thing?"

Truthful looked skeptical. "It could be. But why would God have to do it in a tent, or in any building for that matter? I don't remember that happening in the Book. Why not go into the streets of Megachurch and heal people? It sounds a little suspicious to me."

"Perhaps so, but it might be that the Lord is using a different strategy for different times. Let's go in. I have been walking all day, and it is late. I could use a little time to rest. At the very least, they could tell us where we could find a bed for the night."

There was a long line to enter the tent, and it was moving slowly. The line was filled with people in wheelchairs and on crutches. Some had bald heads from chemotherapy. Others were soldiers who had lost limbs in war. Pilgrim noticed a couple of ushers assisting people as they entered the tent. Occasionally they would ask people to fill out cards listing their names and the type of ailment they had. They offered cards to Pilgrim and Truthful, but the companions declined, saying that they were not in need of healing. What they needed was some good Christian fellowship and edification.

"You will find it here, brothers. The Lord is in his holy Tabernacle tonight. I am sure you will see mighty works of God!"

They were excited at the prospect. "Imagine witnessing healing power like in ancient times. I have often wondered why I never see miracles. Perhaps I was just not in the right place."

They entered the Tabernacle and heard organ music playing. It was not like any church organ they had ever heard. It sounded more like the organ music at a ball game or ice skating rink. It swelled and ebbed with emotion. A woman on the stage had her head back, singing her heart out. A choir swayed behind her. At the close of her song, the crowd cheered, shouting "Amen" and "Hallelujah."

Ben Hinny took the stage dressed in a white suit. He yelled into his mike. "Are you ready to witness the healing power of the Lord?" The audience roared affirmatively.

Then Pilgrim and Truthful witnessed the most amazing things they had ever seen. People were overcome with the power of God, falling to the ground under the influence of the Holy Spirit. Luckily there was always one of the evangelist's assistants ready to lower then gently to the ground. People were healed! Legs were lengthened. Cancer was cured. Migraines disappeared. Hearing was restored. People in wheelchairs stood and pranced around the stage.

But Truthful had some doubts. It was always people with invisible ailments that were healed. There was no way to confirm that it was real. What about the amputees? Did the Lord not love them and want to heal them? What about the boy in the wheelchair with a spinal injury? What about the man with the severe burns over his face and arms? If there was anyone in need of healing it was them? But none of them were brought to the stage. In fact not one of the people that Truthful and Pilgrim had seen in line was healed. "What do you think about these healings, Pilgrim?"

"I am skeptical. I need evidence, and I do not see any. In the Valley of the Shadow of Death I learned a lesson called Occam's Razor. It states that the simplest explanation is most likely the correct one. If I had to choose between whether God is really healing these people or that the evangelist and his staff are pretending to heal people, the latter explanation is the most likely."

The offering plates were being passed around, as the organ swelled and the Evangelist crooned. "You have seen the mighty power of God tonight! The Lord has given. Now it is your chance to give to the Lord."

"This is too much for me," Pilgrim fumed. "The Lord and his apostles never asked for money from those they healed. This is not the Lord's doing. Let's get out of here!"

Pilgrim had the impulse to overturn the offering plates in anger, but then he remembered what happened to his friend Religious, and he thought better of it. "I want nothing to do with this place. I would not accept a place to sleep for the night, even if they offered, which I doubt very much they would. I would rather sleep under the stars than under this tent." They left the Miracle Tabernacle and did not stop walking until the city lights of Megachurch were far behind them.

PART 7
THE FOUR HORSEMEN

They found a place to sleep in a barn a couple of miles outside of town. An elderly couple, who lived in the nearby cottage, discovered them early the next morning while doing their chores. They fed them a hearty breakfast of pancakes and fresh eggs, and saw them on their way. Pilgrim commented to Truthful that these folks were the most Christian people they had met on the Way.

"They never once mentioned our Lord or the Book, but their actions and attitude proclaimed the gospel more powerfully than words," observed Truthful.

They walked for a several miles without seeing another soul. Each hour they came closer to a mountain range, which the elderly couple had identified as the Mystic Mountains. A cloud of dust was visible in the distance and began drawing closer. It looked like a dust devil or sandstorm, but it seemed to follow the road. A rumbling noise accompanied it, and the earth trembled.

"Take cover," Pilgrim yelled over the din. While coughing and putting handkerchiefs over their hands and eyes, they took refuge behind a large boulder by the side of the road.

They waited for the unnatural storm to pass, but it did not. It simply stopped. The dust settled, and they heard the sound of horses snorting. They looked around the side of the boulder to find four horses and riders. The horses were white, sorrel, black, and a gray. The riders did not look like any equestrians that Pilgrim had ever seen. They did not wear English breeches and coats. Nor did they wear American jeans or cowboy boots. They were dressed in tweed coats with elbow patches, as if they had just stepped from a university classroom.

When the rider of the white horse spoke, it was with an Oxford accent. "Greetings, travelers! We bring you warning that you are in grave danger."

"That is why we hid behind this boulder."

The man looked annoyed. "No, we are not the danger! We are warning you of the danger. Turn around immediately and return to your homes."

"We cannot do that. We are following the Way to the Celestial City. It is true that we have encountered many dangers, toils, and snares. But grace has brought us safe thus far, and we

139

are confident that grace will lead us to our heavenly home."

"That is precisely the problem," the Oxfordian replied. "There is no celestial home. It's a delusion."

"We disagree. We have it on good authority that the Land of Light lies just beyond those mountains and across a mighty river."

"We have been beyond the mountains," coughed the man on the ashen mare. "I have crossed the mountains and stood on the bank of the river of which you speak. There is nothing beyond the river but death." The other two nodded in agreement.

Pilgrim and Truthful looked at each other with concern. "May we ask who you are, so we know whether to trust your words?"

"We are known as the Four Horsemen of the New Atheism. We travel this road warning people about religion. It poisons everything."

"You are atheists?"

"New Atheists."

"What makes you different than the old atheists, whose books I have read?"

"I am glad to hear that you have read some of our colleague's books. That means you have an open mind. To answer your question, what makes us different is our attitude. Atheists of long ago were too timid and too respectful of falsehood. We, on the other hand, do not suffer fools gladly. Theism has caused too much harm in the world to go unchallenged any longer. It has led billions of people to commit countless crimes against humanity. Furthermore it has inspired many pilgrims – like yourselves - to travel this Way to their death. We want to put an end to this evil."

"So you say there is no Lord?"

"That is correct."

"Can you prove it?" asked Pilgrim.

"Of course not! No one can prove that something does not exist. You cannot prove that there is not a celestial teapot orbiting the sun somewhere between Earth and Mars.[14] You cannot prove that there is no tooth fairy or Santa Claus. You cannot prove that the Flying Spaghetti Monster did not create the world with his noodly appendages. You cannot prove a negative."

"That is true," said Truthful thoughtfully.

"But there is no evidence that such a being as your Lord actually exists," added the horsemen on the sorrel.

"We have faith he does," replied Pilgrim.

"Faith?" scoffed the first horseman. "Faith is nothing more than believing in something without evidence – or even in spite of contrary evidence."

"Surely a good God must exist, even though we do not have sufficient evidence to prove his existence. There is a reason God does not provide proof of his existence. If we had proof, then we would not be free to believe. We wouldn't need faith. God hides himself in order to preserve our freedom to believe in him. He does not want robots, he wants followers with free will."

"You mean he wants slaves. That is what the apostle Paul called himself and his fellow Christians – slaves of Christ. Furthermore what makes you think that God is good?"

"That is what my pastor taught me in our church in the Shadowlands. He used to say repeatedly that God is good all the time, and all the time God is good."

"On the contrary. God is not good. The God of the Old Testament is arguably the most unpleasant character in all fiction: jealous and proud of it; a petty, unjust, unforgiving control-freak; a vindictive, bloodthirsty ethnic cleanser; a misogynistic, homophobic, racist, infanticidal, genocidal, filicidal, pestilential, megalomaniacal, sadomasochistic, capriciously malevolent bully."[15]

"That seems pretty harsh."

"Harsh. Not at all. It is accurate! Have you read your Book?"

"Cover to cover," stated Pilgrim.

"Did not your God personally kill - or order the killing of - millions of people according to the Book?"

"Well, yes he did. But he had good reasons. Furthermore he had the right to do it because he is God!"

"Might makes right! That is God's excuse for committing crimes against humanity. Because God is almighty he can do whatever he wants, and it is automatically called 'good,' whether it is murdering everyone on earth with a flood or ordering his kings to commit genocide."

Pilgrim had never thought about it that way. "Well what about the New Testament. The God of the New Testament is a God of unconditional love. It says, 'God is Love.'"

"What about the Book of Revelation? That is in the New Testament, and it describes horrendous things that God is planning to do to people on earth! What about hell? That is a New Testament doctrine. It is not found in the Old Testament. It was introduced by Jesus himself. Hell is the eternal torture of billions of people. There is no way that hell can be construed as love. It is evil. If God were real, he would be convicted of war crimes."

Pilgrim winced. "So you say there is no good God?"

"There is not one speck of evidence suggesting there is such a being."

"What about this marvelous, intricate universe that we live in? Surely the wonder of the cosmos requires a Creator."

"No, it doesn't."

"Why not? Something must have started this universe going. Everything has a cause. Even scientists admit that the universe began with the Big Bang over 13 billion years ago. Someone must have started it all going. That First Cause is God!"

"If everything has a cause, then who – or what – caused God?"

"God doesn't have a cause. He is the First Cause."

"If God didn't have a cause, then you have contradicted your statement that everything has a cause. If you can imagine a God that doesn't need a cause, why not just postulate that the universe doesn't need a cause. Why add a God into the equation?"

"But life is too beautiful, intricate, and complicated to have originated by chance. There must be an Intelligent Designer behind it all."

"No there doesn't. Gradual changes over billions of years can account for the evolution of life on this planet."

"What about all the good that has been done in the name of God over the centuries?"

"What about all the evil that has been done in the name of God over the centuries? Do you really want to open that can of worms?"

Pilgrim and Truthful were silent. "I still believe in God," mumbled Pilgrim to Truthful.

"Me too, but I also want to believe only what is true. What if these horsemen are right? If what they say is true, I must believe what is true, regardless of the consequences. I will have to think about this some more."

Having felt like they had fulfilled their purpose in bringing a ray of rationality into the dark minds of some lost souls, the Brights (for that is what they called themselves) rode off to warn other pilgrims of the folly of their quest. Pilgrim and Truthful continued on their way, but their pace was noticeably less spirited than before.

THE DETOUR

As they traveled along the Way, the road became noticeably rougher. The Way here seemed like a dry river bed, filled with rocks and boulders. Often they had to use both hands to clamber over rocks. More than once the travelers stumbled and fell. They bruised their legs and twisted their ankles on the rocks.

"I knew the Way was going to be strait and narrow, but I did not know it was going to be stony and rocky." Truthful complained. "I can hardly walk on this path, if it truly is a path! Are you sure we did not accidently stray from the Way awhile back? Perhaps the Four Horsemen distracted us, and we got off the path by accident."

Pilgrim agreed that the road was much harder than he expected. "Look over there. There is a grassy path running parallel to this road – if you can call it that. And there is a sign. Let's go see what it says." So they hobbled over to inspect the sign. It read, "Detour."

"The Way must have been washed out in a storm, and this detour built to help pilgrims. It certainly looks a hell of a lot – I mean, a heck of a lot - better."

Truthful was not convinced. "I am not so sure. It may be a dead end or lead to an entirely different destination."

"But look how it runs beside the rocky road for as far as we can see. Let's give it a try. If it deviates too far from the Way, then we can always return. In the meantime it will give our feet and shins a break. And we will make much better time!" So they traveled along the grassy way. The further they went the more glad they were that that they had made this choice.

After a while they noticed a fellow traveler up ahead of them. "Wait up!" they called. The figure did exactly that. His name, they found out, was Optimist.

"Do you know where this detour leads?"

"To the Heavenly City, of course! Where else would it lead?"

"You see," Pilgrim smirked to Truthful, "I was right. I am so glad we took this detour. And I am very grateful to the Lord for showing it to us."

They walked all day. As dark began to fall, Truthful stopped. "Hey, where is the Way? I don't see it any longer."

"It was over there to the right not long ago."

"How long ago did you last see it?"

"Well, I'm not sure. I was enjoying this path and our fellowship with Optimist so much that I did not pay attention to the Way."

"Stop worrying, you two!" Optimist interjected. "It is a detour after all. I am sure that this path will rejoin the main road further on."

He strode head of them, while Pilgrim and Truthful stopped to discuss the pros and cons of continuing or going back the way they came. Soon Optimist was out of sight.

They decided to continue on the grassy path until nightfall, then make camp. They would look for the Way in the morning. The sun set, and the darkness deepened. The two were about to make camp when they heard a scream up ahead. "That sounds like Optimist!" They made their way carefully in the dark until the path abruptly ended at the edge of a cliff.

"If we had been walking normally, we would have fallen right in!"

"That must be what happened to Optimist."

They called down into the darkness and listened for a response. There was nothing but silence. They dropped a rock into the abyss, and waited for the sound of it hitting the bottom. It took several seconds.

Pilgrim moaned. "If he fell down there, he is gone. No one could have survived this drop."

"So what do we do now? We do not even know where we are. If only we had stayed on the Way!"

Pilgrim agreed. "It is all my fault. But who could have known that this detour would have led us this far astray?"

Just then it began to rain, accompanied by lightning and thunder. They slowly and carefully retraced their steps, but the path became a torrent of water. They were forced to leave the detour and seek higher ground, with only flashes of lightning to guide their way. After a while they saw a small hunting cabin and took shelter there. They decided to leave at the break of dawn, and they soon fell asleep.

THE DARK KNIGHT OF THE SOUL

It so happened that the cabin belonged to a man called the Dark Knight who lived in the nearby Castle of Despair with his wife Acedia. The Dark Knight had the habit of walking his property every morning at dawn. When he came to his hunting cabin, he noticed that the door had been opened recently. He entered and saw the two men. He woke them with a shout. "What are you doing trespassing on my property?"

They explained to him that they were pilgrims on the Way, and that they had become lost in the storm and dark. They had taken refuge in the cabin, believing that the owner would not begrudge them refuge from the storm. "We did not touch a thing. We only slept on the floor. We did not even light a fire, even though we were cold and wet."

"I see. Come with me."

They followed, not knowing what was in store for them, but feeling obliged to accompany the Knight because they had wronged him. When they reached his castle he called two of his guards, Desolation and Abandonment, and ordered them to arrest the two men and put them into the dungeon.

On the way they passed a cavern containing hundreds of skulls and bones. "Whose are these?" they asked. "The bones of pilgrims who trespassed on our master's land," they responded.

They were chained to the wall in the deepest cell and left in the dark. The darkness was so deep and dark that they could not see each other. No sunlight leaked into their cell. No noise reached them from the outside. There was only the occasional rattle of the chains that bound them. Time passed without any way to measure it.

"Paul and Silas sang and prayed when they were in the prison of Philippi, and the Lord delivered them," said Truthful. So they prayed. They sang songs and hymns of praise to God. Days passed without food or water. They grew weary of praying. It seemed to have no effect. They despaired and wished to die. They even thought of killing themselves, but there was no way to do it.

"I think the Dark Knight has forgotten about us. I also fear that the Lord himself has abandoned us, perhaps as punishment for forsaking the Way. This prison is a living hell," moaned Truthful.

Pilgrim prayed to the Lord in his distress in groans too deep for words. Then words tumbled forth, disjointed and full of anguish.

"I am in the darkness. Lord, my God, who am I that you should forsake me? I am the child of your love, yet now I have become as the most hated one. The one you have thrown away as unwanted, unloved. I call, I cling, I want, and there is no one to answer. When I try to raise my thoughts to heaven, there is such convicting emptiness that those very thoughts return like sharp knives and hurt my very soul. Love. The word — it brings nothing. I am told God lives in me, and yet the reality of darkness and coldness and emptiness is so great that nothing touches my soul."[16]

Truthful responded with a lament of his own:

"I feel a terrible emptiness,
a feeling of the absence of God.
They say people in hell suffer eternal pain
because of the loss of God.
In my soul I feel this terrible pain of loss,
of God not wanting me, of God not being God,
of God not really existing.
That terrible longing keeps growing, and I feel as if
something will break in me one day.
Heaven from every side is closed.

I feel like refusing God.
Pray for me that I may not turn a Judas to
Jesus in this painful darkness."[17]

The two travelers prayed and prayed. Three days
and three nights passed, but it seemed like an
eternity. They recited the words of Job.

"Why is light given to him who is in misery,
    and life to the bitter in soul,
who long for death, but it comes not,
    and dig for it more than for hidden treasures,
who rejoice exceedingly
    and are glad when they find the grave?
Why is light given to a man whose way is
hidden,
    whom God has hedged in?
For my sighing comes instead of my bread,
    and my groanings are poured out like water.
For the thing that I fear comes upon me,
    and what I dread befalls me.
I am not at ease, nor am I quiet;
    I have no rest, but trouble comes."[18]

They prayed the words of the psalmist and of
their Lord. "My God, my God! Why hast thou
forsaken me?"

Finally a pinpoint of light appeared in the
darkness.

"Do you see that?" asked Truthful.

"It is nothing but a trick of the eyes. We have been too long in darkness."

"No, there is a small crack between the stones behind you. It only was revealed when you moved slightly."

Pilgrim twisted and found the crack between the foundation stones of the dungeon. He dug at the crevice until his fingernails broke and blood began to flow from his fingers, making it difficult to dig. Finally he touched metal. "I think it may be a key!"

He dug for another hour, until he could grasp the key and remove it. "This must have been hidden by a previous prisoner."

He placed the key in his manacles, and they fell open. The same with the shackles on his feet. He quickly freed Truthful. They went to the cell door, and found it unlocked.

"I guess they never thought anyone could escape from the chains, so they did not bother to lock the door," Truthful speculated.

Within minutes they were out of the dungeon and into the light. Fortunately for them it was the beginning of dawn. Otherwise the brightness of the sun would have blinded them. As quickly as they could, they found their way back to the hut and then to the grassy path. In the distance they heard the roar of the Dark Knight, who had discovered that the door to his dungeon was open and his prisoners had escaped.

Pilgrim and Truthful ran as fast as they could back to the King's Highway where they had first taken the Detour. They paused long enough to scratch a warning onto the sign, so that other pilgrims would know that the detour leads to death and despair. They also placed the key on the top of the sign.

"I wonder if that will deter other travelers and save them from the dangers we suffered."

"I hope so" replied Truthful, "but I suspect that the Dark Knight's domain must be traversed one way or the other."

PART 8
THE MYSTIC MOUNTAINS

Pilgrim and Truthful walked the Way until they came to the Mystic Mountains, which belong to the Lord. As they approached the foothills, they saw gardens of vegetables and flowers. There were orchards and vineyards as well. They drank from a spring which flowed from a Rock. They rested for a while, bathing in the pool that gathered at the spring. They ate from the orchards surrounding the river, whose source was that spring, believing that the owner would not mind because the fruit was so abundant.

In the distance they could see shepherds feeding their flocks upon the lush grass of that land. In time the two pilgrims, refreshed from their respite approached the shepherds, who were leaning on their staffs.

"Whose mountains are these and whose are the sheep that feed upon them?"

One of the shepherds answered, "This is Emmanuel's Land. These mountains are within sight of his city. The sheep on a thousand hills are his, as are all the animals of the forest."

"Is this the way to the Celestial City?"

"You are on the right road."

"How much farther do we have to go?"

"It is too far for anyone but those who will get there."

"Is the rest of the way safe or dangerous?"

"It is safe for those who will arrive, but all others will fail."

"Your words are cryptic," responded Truthful. "Is there anyone who can speak to us more directly or perhaps guide us on our Way through the mountains?"

"We can point out the path, but the Lord will be your guide."

"Is there is a place where we can spend the night before we attempt to cross this rugged terrain?"

"The Lord of these mountains has instructed us to entertain strangers. You are welcome in our tents."

The shepherds questioned them about their journey. Where did you come from? How did you enter the Way? What trials and temptations did you encounter? How did you persevere? When the shepherds were satisfied that they were sincere travelers on the Way, they embraced them and said "Welcome to the Mystic Mountains!"

The shepherd named Hospitality led them to their tents, and spread out a table before them. "We would be honored if you would stay for a while with us, to regain your strength for the trip to come. Pilgrim and Truthful said they would we honored to stay for a few days and learn about Emmanuel's Land and the inhabitants of the mountains. Because it was already late, they fell asleep soon after they ate.

HILL OF PRIDE

In the morning the shepherds invited them to walk with them. They took them to the top of a hill called Pride, which was very steep on its far side. They asked them to look down over the edge to the bottom. There they saw the remains of many people who had fallen and were lying in crumpled heaps.

"What does this mean?" asked Pilgrim.

One shepherd quoted, "Pride goes before destruction, and a haughty spirit before a fall."

Another explained, "These are ones who were proud of getting this far on their spiritual pilgrimage. Therefore they got no further. Some thought they were saints or even the Messiah. Others started their own religions. At the bottom are the bones of popes and cardinals, televangelists and faith-healers, theologians and philosophers."

Mount Fear

Next they took them to the top of a mountain called Fear. The shepherds instructed them to look into the distance. They could make out several men and women wandering among some tombs. The people walked with arms outstretched, stumbling as they walked. It was clear that they were blind.

"What is this?" asked Pilgrim.

"Back on the path did you see an alternative way called Detour?"

They responded cautiously, "Yes, we did."

"It is a path that leads to the Castle of the Dark Knight. These people that you see came on pilgrimage just as you have. But when the Way got rough they chose the easy way. Eventually they were captured by the Dark Knight, where they were kept in his dungeon for forty days and forty nights. At the end of those forty days, if they had not taken their own lives, he gave them over to his wife Acedia, who put out their eyes and let them go. Now they wander among the tombs of the dead."

Pilgrim and Truthful shuddered and looked at each other with horror, knowing that this would have been their fate if not for the grace of God. But they said nothing to the shepherds about their experience.

DOORS OF PERCEPTION

Next the shepherds took them to the bottom of the mountain. There in the side of the mountain was a door. The shepherds opened the door quietly. The pilgrims peeked in and saw that it was very dark and smoky. They could hear chants coming from within.

"What is this place?"

"This is one of the Doors of Perception, considered by some to be a short-cut to the Celestial City."

"What is the odor coming forth from this place?"

"That is the smoke of opium and cocaine, but those are the least of the substances consumed in this place. Those people most serious about taking this path use peyote, psilocybin and LSD. Hallucinogens like these have been used by religions around the world for thousands of years."

"Do they work? Is this a shortcut?"

"You can see for yourself. This is a cave, not a tunnel. This leads only to fantasies of the mind. These visions can be very enticing. They seem to transport a soul beyond the Mystic Mountains to the Land of Light, but in reality the people remain in a Cave of Darkness. Many have lost their minds in this place, never to emerge again."

The shepherds closed the door gently so as not to disturb the dreams of those within.

"Come, I will show you the highest of the Mystic Mountains."

The shepherds donned warm clothing and provided the pilgrims with the same. The shepherds looked more like Sherpas now. It took several days of trekking until they reached what the shepherds called their base camp.

"These mountains are far vaster than I ever imagined," exclaimed Truthful.

"Indeed, they are higher than the Himalayas. We will stay here for a while to become accustomed to the altitude."

After a few days they continued to an outlook where the shepherd guides showed them a panorama of majestic mountains. "From here we will point out to you some of the major peaks."

Mount Transfiguration

"Over there," said one of their guides, pointing to the nearest peak, "is Mount Transfiguration."

"I remember that from the Book," Truthful nodded. "That is where our Lord was clothed in white and light in the presence of some of his disciples."

"Correct. He was transfigured before them. The disciples saw a vision of Moses and Elijah, and God spoke from heaven. You will also remember that Peter did not want to leave that mountain. He wanted to build three tabernacles on the summit and dwell there always. That is exactly what people have done ever since. Look closer."

The shepherd handed Truthful a small telescope that he had brought with him. Truth peered through the spyglass and saw structures on that summit. It looked like a community. "Who are these people?"

"These are those who spend their days seeking transcendental experiences. They fast and pray. They chant and meditate. They yearn for mountaintop experiences and never go into the valleys where the human needs are. Those who live on Mount Transfiguration desire nothing more than spiritual experiences, which they induce by means of spiritual practices. They succeed in having all sorts of strange visions. They have Out of Body Experiences, Past Life Regression, and Near Death Experiences. They even have encounters with UFOs. Some of them have migrated to Mount Carmel, which is that peak next to it," said the shepherd, pointing to another mountain. "There they cut themselves like the prophets of Baal. They engage in shamanistic practices, sweat lodges, and fire walking. They push themselves to the limits of physical endurance for the purpose of entering into trances and achieving spiritual experiences."

"When do they stop?"

"They never stop, and they never continue to the Celestial City. Like Esau they have exchanged their birthright for a mess of pottage."

"That is sad."

"That is not the saddest sight you will see in these mountains. Let me show you more."

THE LAMASERY

They traveled a few miles deeper into the mountains where they stopped on a ridge with a view of the highest peaks. The guide pointed out a peak upon which was built a majestic lamasery. The structure was surrounded with colorful prayer flags. Prayer Wheels could be heard whirling in the wind. Walking around the grounds were monks clothed in saffron robes.

"What is that place?"

"It is the Tibetan Temple of the Dead."

"You mean that is part of the afterlife?"

"No, they are physically alive but their end is death. They believe that the wind prays for them and that wheels chant for them. They have created elaborate mythologies and rituals, which they adhere to religiously."

Pilgrim and Truthful were startled to see something lift off from the lamasery and fly away. "What was that?"

"That was the Dalai Lama flying off to engage in one of his Charm Offensives. He has mastered the ancient art of the Disarming Smile. All he has to do is laugh, and people give him money. I have met him, and I have to say that he is a very nice man. That is the danger. Niceness can lull a person into spiritual complacency."

Shangri-La

They followed the flight of the helicopter with their eyes and noticed that it flew over a green valley, which seemed very out of place in these mountains.

Pilgrim pointed. "What is that over there? It looks like a lush valley in the middle of these snow-capped mountains."

"That is Shangri-La, made famous by the pilgrim James Hilton, who once traveled this way as you have. Look more closely at it through the telescope." He handed it to Pilgrim.

"I seem to see rows of colorful flowers."

"Those are not flowers. Those are people on their yoga mats. If you look closely you will see others practicing Reiki, aromatherapy, and homeopathy. When the wind blows in the right direction you can catch a whiff of their incense.

They even have their own Trader Joes and Starbucks, although most prefer herbal tea."

"What is that pattern located in the center of the valley?"

"That is a labyrinth. They like to walk in circles. It gives them the illusion that they are making spiritual progress. If only they would get out of there and back onto the Way! But they have given up on the Way. They view it as too narrow and confining."

A shepherd directed the attention of the two travelers to the highest peak in the range of the Mystic Mountains.

MOUNT ADVAITA

"Do you see that peak there, whose summit is in the clouds? That is Mount Advaita, but some call it Nonduality Mountain. It is the farthest that anyone has traveled in these mountains."

"It is so far away that I cannot see anyone on the summit."

"Yes, that is the nature of that mountain. It is nearly always nestled in clouds."

"Do people live there?"

"Yes ... and no. They are people but they no longer consider themselves to be persons. They have come to think that they are not individuals and never were. For them all is One. There is no distinction between this and that. They like to talk in riddles. Unfortunately very few can live in the rarified atmosphere of that peak. Most live in the valley below called Vedanta Vale, also called Guru Gorge, where they live out their days hoping to catch a glimpse of the summit on clear days. They sit at the feet of spiritual teachers and dream of one day ascending the mountain."

"Do any of them continue on the Way to the Land of Light?"

"Oh, no. They have forgotten that they are on a pilgrimage. They believe there is nowhere to go. They no longer believe there is a Way or a Land of Light. Light and Darkness are the same to them. They are forever lost in the mists of the Mystic Mountains."

"Is there any more you can show us?"

"Yes. We have saved the best for last."

Inspiration Point

The travelers were guided back the way they had come. Below the hill called Pride, the shepherds stopped at a knoll called Inspiration Point.

"From here you can view the Way, which winds through the western edge of the Mystic Mountains. In the distance – if you look closely - you can just make out something that shines with iridescence in the sun. Do you see it?"

"Yes, I do!"

"So do I! It is beautiful even at this great distance."

"Those are the Pearly Gates that lead into the Celestial City. You are within sight of your goal. May the Lord guide you on your journey."

PART 9

THE LAND OF CAUTION

The two friends descended the mountains and followed the Way toward the Celestial City. In a few miles the Way joined with another road. A road sign identified the crossroads as the Land of Caution. At the intersection stood a fine house with a young man standing out front. They could tell by his clothing and the size of his home that he was a wealthy person. Upon seeing the pilgrims he invited them to sit on his front porch for rest and refreshment. Since it was a hot day, they agreed.

RICH YOUNG RULER

As they sat in rocking chairs drinking a cool drink, they conversed about the Way. The young man spoke eloquently about the importance of morality while traveling the Way. "There are many temptations along the way, but I have conquered them all," he crowed.

He boasted that he had kept all the Lord's commandments all this life. He asked the pilgrims if they had done the same. They admitted that they both had fallen short, but that they had been forgiven of their sins by the Lord. The young man nodded sadly.

"May we ask your name?" the men inquired.

"I am known as the Rich Young Ruler."

"You bear the same name as a man in the Book who was also traveling the Way. Are you he?"

"I am indeed."

"How did you get this far? We are told in the Book that you were not able to enter by the Gate because of your many possessions."

"I have found another way - the road you see here to your right. It is a much more reasonable path than the way you have come."

"Why did you not enter by the Gate?"

"You mean the door they call the Eye of the Needle? That was far too narrow for my liking. I would have had to give up my wealth and title. Even though I love the Lord, I knew in my heart that it was not necessary to do something as drastic as that. I can worship and serve the Lord just as well in my fine house in my fine clothing. People around here respect me greatly. I have financed the building of a large church just down the road in the town of Caution. In fact they elected me chairman of the Board of Trustees. You should come and worship with us this Sunday."

"We are on the way to the Celestial City. As fine as your house and your church are, they are not the Celestial City. Forgive me for saying so," said Truthful, "but I believe that your wealth and success have hindered you from reaching the goal of the spiritual life."

"You are mistaken. Everyone knows that one cannot reach the Celestial City in this lifetime. I am perfectly content to serve the Lord in my own humble way while on earth and see him in the next life."

"I do not believe that you will see him at all. You must obey the Lord. He has told you to sell all that you have and give it to the poor and follow Him."

The Rich Young Ruler grimaced. "I see that you are religious fanatics. Why are there so many extremists on the Way? Aren't there any sensible believers in the world anymore?"

Then he turned his back on the pilgrims and went into his house. Sensing that this was an invitation to leave, they put down their glasses and walked down the front steps. As they stepped onto the road, they could hear weeping coming from within the house.

"If only he could find it in his heart to return and enter by the narrow gate," said Pilgrim.

Truthful sighed. "It is easier for a camel to go through the eye of a needle than for a rich man to enter the kingdom of God."

FAMILY WOMAN

A few more miles down the road the travelers heard laughter.

"Where is that coming from? It sounds like people filled with love and joy. Perhaps we are nearer than we thought to the Celestial City!"

"No, it appears to be coming from down that long driveway. Let's turn aside and see who these people are."

Truthful was hesitant. "I don't know. You know what happened last time we took a detour."

"I promise that we will come right back to the Way in a few minutes. Don't these people sound like they are filled with the joy of the Lord? What could be the harm in saying hello to them?"

Pilgrim started off down the driveway, and Truthful reluctantly followed. Soon they came to a large farmhouse. There was a gaggle of children playing in the yard. As soon as they approached, the children ran up to them smiling. One little girl gave Truthful a big hug, which took the scowl off his face immediately.

A woman, who appeared to be in her forties, came out of the house wiping her hands on her apron. The aroma of fresh bread followed her across the yard.

"Welcome pilgrims. We do not get many visitors here. Come a take a load off your feet. Is there anything I can get you?"

"Just a little water would be fine. We had refreshment a short time ago at the house of the Rich Young Ruler."

"Very nice man," she replied, "and very generous to our church."

This time it was Pilgrim's turn to scowl. "You attend his church?"

"Yes, we do. It is the only church in these parts. But we are not rich like he is. We gave up all claim to possessions when we entered through the Gate."

Pilgrim breathed a sigh of relief. They followed the woman to the porch where they sat down on a porch swing.

After they had received glasses of cold water from the spring in the yard, Pilgrim asked, "How is it that you have settled here and not continued to the Celestial City."

"I met my husband while traveling on the Way. He helped me though the Valley of the Shadow of Death, and I fell in love with him. We were married in the church of the Rich Young Ruler, and decided to settle right here. We have a wonderful life. The Lord has blessed us with seven beautiful children. We grow all our own food. We are very active in our church. We have gone on several mission trips to the Shadowlands, and I volunteer at the Crisis Pregnancy Center."

"But you never resumed your journey to the Celestial City."

"No, our family and church obligations prohibit us. 'Family First' is our motto."

"That is very commendable, but are you not putting your family above the Lord?"

She smiled. "We love the Lord by loving our family. We are raising good, moral, God-fearing children. Would you like to hear them sing Edelweiss?"

"No, that is alright. But didn't the Lord warn us not to put anyone before Him, even our families. I seem to remember that he said, 'Whoever loves father or mother more than me is not worthy of me, and whoever loves son or daughter more than me is not worthy of me.'"[19]

"Yes, our Lord did say that. But our pastor teaches that he did not mean that literally."

"On another occasion he said it even stronger," added Truthful. "He said, 'If anyone comes to me and does not hate his own father and mother and wife and children and brothers and sisters, yes, and even his own life, he cannot be my disciple.'"[20]

"He obviously did not mean that literally. He was speaking in hyperbole. He was all about love, not hate."

"Jesus may not want us to hate anyone, but he called his disciples from their families. They said to him, 'We have left our homes to follow you.'"[21]

"Yes, but..."

"Jesus did not marry nor have a family. Neither did the apostle Paul. In fact Paul said it was better not to marry."[22]

"That is true, but I am sure our Lord loved his earthly family. He was all about family values."

Pilgrim responded, "Jesus said, 'Who is my mother, and who are my brothers?' And stretching out his hand toward his disciples, he said, 'Here are my mother and my brothers! For whoever does the will of my Father in heaven is my brother and sister and mother.'"[23]

Truthful interrupted. "Have you and your husband ever thought about bringing your whole family with you to the Celestial City?"

"We have talked about it. But our life is here, and we are very content. Besides the Way is too dangerous for children, and we have an obligation to keep them safe. Several of them have not reached the Age of Accountability yet."

She glanced nervously over her shoulder. "Oh, my goodness. I have forgotten all about my bread. It will burn it for sure! Nice to meet you," she said as she raced into the house. "Stop in and see us on your way back!"

"'On your way back?' muttered Pilgrim. "I am not planning on coming back. This is a one way trip, not a holiday excursion."

"As nice as these people are, I think we need to get back on the road," decided Truthful.

"Or she might try to set us up with some of her friends at church," smiled Pilgrim.

They put down their glasses and stepped off the porch. As they walked down the driveway, they heard music coming from the house. They turned to see the seven children lined up on the porch singing, "So long, farewell, auf wiedersehen, adieu."

Goatman

The two walked for hours, finally stopping to rest at the edge of a copse of trees near a brook. They drank from the flowing water and rested in the shade.

"What is that?" said Pilgrim, pointing.

"What are you talking about?"

"There in the trees. It looks like an animal of some sort."

As if on cue, a strange creature emerged from the undergrowth.

"Mr. Tumnus!" shouted Pilgrim.

"No, I am not Tumnus," the creature said with a scowl, "and this is not Narnia. Sometimes I wish Jack had never written those books!"

"But you look just like the character in the Chronicles of Narnia. You are even wearing a scarf."

"Please notice that mine is brown, not red like in the books. What faun would wear a red scarf? He would not blend into the wood ... except in autumn of course."

"I'm sorry. You are exactly how I pictured Tumnus."

"That is because the professor patterned his fictional character after me. Therefore it is understandable that you would be confused."

"May I ask your name?"

"It is Gida. I would add that I am much more famous than that Narnian creature. I am not in a children's tale. I am in the Book!"

"Where exactly are you mentioned in the Book?"

"The Lord told a story about the Sheep and the Goats. Do you remember it?"

"Of course I do. It is one of the most powerful scenes in all of scripture. The Good Shepherd will separate the sheep from the goats, based on what they did ... or did not do ... in life. But if you are one of those goats, what are you doing here? According to the Lord the goats are thrown into eternal fire."

"No, no, no! He was just talking about something that MIGHT happen in the future."

"You mean WILL happen in the future."

"No, I mean MIGHT. When he hears all the facts, the Shepherd may decide differently. There are extenuating circumstances that the Lord did not take into consideration when telling that story."

"For instance?"

"There are good reasons why the sheep do all those good deeds and goats do not."

"Please explain."

"Gladly. The Book says that the sheep feed the hungry, welcome strangers, clothe the naked, tend the sick, and visit prisoners. Right?"

"Correct."

"But it does not explain that poor people are hungry because they are lazy. That is why I do not give them food. It doesn't help them in the long run. It keeps them dependent on welfare. They need to get off their lazy butts and earn their keep. Doesn't the Book say, 'He who does not work, neither shall he eat?' By not feeding them I am helping them get on their feet. The Book says, 'God helps those who help themselves.'"

"No it doesn't. Actually Ben Franklin said that."

"Well, it is still true, whoever said it. Furthermore I do not welcome strangers because they are dangerous. 'Stranger danger' my mother called it. Most strangers are illegal immigrants, you know. And immigrants are all terrorists, drug dealers, criminals, and rapists. I am sure there may be a few good ones, but you can never be too careful. Plus they are taking all our jobs."

"How about the sick, why do you not visit them?"

"I might get sick! HIV and leprosy and things like that. They are highly contagious!"

"Actually they are not."

"Well, there are plenty of other contagious diseases. I read recently that a hospital is one of the most dangerous places for healthy people. All those superbugs and things."

"How about people in prison. I can guess why you do not visit them. All drug dealers, criminals, and rapists, right?"

"Why else would they be in prison?"

"Then why did the sheep in the story help all those people?"

"Sheep aren't too smart, you know. Always getting fleeced. They get lost easily and have to be carried by the shepherd. They can't climb at all. Not like us goats! I never understood why the Lord preferred sheep over goats and used them as examples of believers. They are dumb animals who can't think for themselves. Goats are so much wiser."

"Woe unto them that are wise in their own eyes...."[24]

"What was that you said?"

"Nothing. Well, we have to be going now. See you at the Last Judgment." The two pilgrims abruptly turned and continued on their way.

"If you make it to Aslan's Land, say 'Hi' to Lucy for me," Gida mocked. "And Reepicheep!" he added chuckling

A little way down the road Truthful spoke. "To be honest I don't think I am much different than Gida."

"How so?"

"I don't really aid the poor. I give some money to relief organizations on occasion. When a hurricane or flood strikes I will text a few dollars to the Red Cross, but that is the extent of my care for the needy. I spend more on my cellphone service than I do on aid to the poorest of the poor. I have never invited a stranger into my home. I admit I am afraid of people who look and speak differently than I do. The only people I have ever visited in the hospital were family and friends. And I have never been inside a prison. I guess I am a goat."

"Now that you put it that way, I see what you mean," Pilgrim replied. "I have helped out at the church soup kitchen and homeless shelter, but it never cost me more than a few hours a month. I marched in a protest of the government's immigration policy, but I have never personally done anything for immigrants. Like you, I have never known a prisoner. I guess we need to look at our own lives before we condemn the goats. Take the plank out of our own eyes, and all that."

"Did you ever notice that in the story of the sheep and goats there is no mention of faith? It is all what you do or don't do."

"That doesn't fit the party line about salvation by grace through faith, does it?"

"No, it doesn't. It reminds me of something that our Lord said in his Sermon on the Mount. He said: 'Not everyone who says to me, "Lord, Lord," will enter the kingdom of heaven, but the one who does the will of my Father who is in heaven. On that day many will say to me, "Lord, Lord, did we not prophesy in your name, and cast out demons in your name, and do many mighty works in your name?" And then will I declare to them, "I never knew you; depart from me, you workers of lawlessness."'"[25]

"It sounds like it is not enough just to believe in Jesus as Lord, even if that is backed up by powerful preaching, ministries and great works."

"Perhaps salvation is not as simple as we thought it was."

CENTURION

They traveled the next few miles in silence, each reexamining their own faith and deeds. They were so deep in thought that they were not paying attention to the road. They nearly bumped into a soldier standing in the middle of the path. He was dressed like a Roman centurion in full armor.

"Halt! In the Name of the King of Kings!" the man ordered.

They halted and gawked at the powerful figure with his drawn sword. "Sir, we are two humble servants of your King on our way to the Capital."

"You are not dressed like his servants. Where is your armor?"

"Do you mean the Full Armor of God that I received at First Baptist Church?" Pilgrim asked. "I am afraid I left that on the ground when I faced Abaddon?"

The centurion looked impressed. "Do you mean to say that you faced the great demon in battle? Even I have not seen him face to face. How did you defeat him?"

"Well, to tell the truth, I saw right through him. He is not real at all – just a creation of my fears. That is why I left my armor and weapons on the battlefield. I did not need them after all."

"Liar! He is a powerful foe of our Lord and King. He would not let anyone go without a fierce fight."

"He did not let me go. I defeated him without violence."

"Impossible! Force is the Way of God. My King is a great warrior. The Book says, 'The Lord is a warrior; the Lord is his name. Pharaoh's chariots and his army He has cast into the sea.'[26] He fought for his people when Joshua entered the Promised Land. He fought for Saul and David and Solomon. 'The LORD will go forth like a warrior. He will arouse His zeal like a man of war. He will utter a shout, yes, He will raise a war cry! He will prevail against His enemies.'"[27]

Truthful responded, "The Book certainly says all those things. But it also says that our Lord is a God of Peace. He send his Son into the world to be the Prince of Peace."

Pilgrim agreed. "I have found that nonviolence is more powerful than the sword. That is why our Lord told Peter to put away his sword, saying, 'For those who live by the sword will perish by the sword.'"[28]

"I have lived by the sword all my life. Our Lord said that he had not found greater faith than mine in all of Israel."[29]

"He was commending your faith, not your choice of careers. Our Lord was clearly a man of nonviolence. He said, 'You have heard that it was said, "An eye for an eye and a tooth for a tooth." But I say to you, Do not resist the one who is evil. But if anyone slaps you on the right cheek, turn to him the other also.... You have heard that it was said, "You shall love your neighbor and hate your enemy." But I say to you, Love your enemies and pray for those who persecute you, so that you may be sons of your Father who is in heaven."[30]

"Perhaps he said that, but I have not found that to be so," replied the soldier. "My experience is that enemies respect only force."

"Force, yes. But soul force, not military force."

"Now you sound like Gandhi or Martin Luther King."

"You know them?"

"I have met them. They have both come this way, and they said exactly what you are saying. I told them the same thing I am telling you."

"Perhaps that is why you have been content to stand your ground here and not continue your journey to the Celestial City," Truthful observed.

The centurion was quiet. "Indeed, I have tried to cross the river ahead, but it meant shedding my armor and sword. That I am unwilling to do."

The three of them stood silently for a few moments, contemplating the gravity of that statement.

"You may pass," the Roman finally said. "Though I may not agree with your ways, you are clearly servants of the King." The two pilgrims walked on.

EVANGELICAL

Around the next corner the travelers met another man. This one was dressed much like them and was about the same age. He had a copy of the Book under his arm, a smile on his face, and he was singing a contemporary worship song that Pilgrim recognized from his church in the Shadowlands. As he got closer he recognized the man. His name was Evangelical. He was a part of the worship team at Pilgrim's church. Upon seeing each other they embraced. Pilgrim introduced him to Truthful and then spend the next half hour catching up.

"It has been a year or more since I last saw you," Pilgrim said. "I had heard that you left for the Celestial City. In fact your example was the inspiration for my own journey. But what are you doing here? I thought for sure that you would havc rcachcd your goal by now."

"Because you are a brother in Christ, I will be honest with you. I made it all the way to the riverbank, but I could not bring myself to cross to the Celestial City."

"Why is that?"

"There are several reasons. One is similar to the Centurion down the road. I also have a problem with making that last journey unarmed." Evangelical pulled out his handgun. "This sidearm has come in handy several times on my journey, and who knows what enemies might dwell beyond the river. There may be pirates on that river or sea monsters under it. I would feel naked without some means of self-defense."

"But if the Lord wants you to lay down your arms for that final leg of the journey, would he not protect you?"

"I would hope so, but I believe it was the Lord who led me to carry this gun in the first place. This is how he protects me – through the Second Amendment."

"You said there were several reasons. What are the others?"

"Not only would I have to leave my handgun behind, but I would have to leave behind my spiritual weapon as well," he said raising his Bible.

"You mean the Sword of the Spirit, which is the Word of God?"[31]

"Yes, I was required to leave behind the Book."

"But if the Author of the Book asked you to do that, then he must have a good reason."

"The Spirit of the Lord told me that I would not need it on the other shore. He said I would hear the Word directly from the mouth of God and would not need the Book. His exact words were: 'when that which is perfect comes, then that which is imperfect shall pass away.'"[32]

"That sounds pretty good to me," chimed in Truthful.

"It sounds scary to me. This Book is the inerrant, infallible Word of God! He would never ask me to abandon it."

"But I thought you said he did exactly that."

"Yes, he did. That is the problem. I am wondering if it was the Voice of the Lord or the voice of the Enemy."

"Can't you tell the difference? They do not sound anything alike to me."

"That is what I thought. But I can't accept that there is any authority higher than the Book."

"What other reason prevented you from crossing the river to the Celestial City?"

"That is where it gets even worse. I was asked to abandon my political principles. 'No Republicans in heaven' were His exact words."

"What?" Pilgrim and Truthful said in unison.

"No Religious Right allowed in the Celestial City."

"Are they all a bunch of liberals over there?"

"No, apparently there are no Democrats there either. No leftists or socialists. We have to leave all of that on this side."

He paused. "There is even more," added Evangelical. "I was asked to give up my beliefs."

"All your beliefs? Including your religious beliefs?"

"Yes. No religion in heaven. No doctrines. Those who would cross over must put aside creeds and dogma and cross the river by faith alone."

Pilgrim paused to ponder that statement. After a few moments Truthful cautiously spoke. "As much as I love truth, I know deep down that truth is not a set of ideas. The Lord is Truth. Is that not what it said over the Gate by which we entered on this Way?"

"Yes. The Lord is the Way, the Truth, and the Life. But the great doctrines of our faith have been our guides for centuries. How can we be asked to put them aside now? Are they not true?"

"Perhaps they are true, but they are not True," responded Truthful. "There is a difference."

"Is there any more?" Pilgrim asked Evangelical warily.

"Yes. We cannot bring our righteousness."

"You have got to be kidding me! Are you sure about that? I thought righteousness was an integral part of the Kingdom of God."

"Yes, God's righteousness, but not our own. I was told that because there is no evil in the City, there is also no good. You can't have one without the other. It is a Land beyond good and evil, beyond truth and falsehood, beyond right and wrong. It is beyond anything we can imagine. In short if we are to travel the final leg of our journey, we have to leave behind everything that defines us, everything that separates us from others and from God."

The three stood in silence. Finally Evangelical spoke. "I found it more than I could stomach. I am a Bible-believing Christian. I am a conservative. I am an evangelical. I am a defender of all that is right and good against all that is wrong. I knew that if I agreed to put aside all these things I would never make it across that river alive. Even if I did, I would no longer be myself on the other side. Without these values, who am I? What am I? That is why I remain here and watch others go on."

Pilgrim shook his head in empathy. "I understand completely. If what you say is true – and I know you are a person of the highest integrity – then I may stay with you. But first I have to see the river for myself."

"I think you will agree with me," said Evangelical, "for I know you are a genuine believer. I hope you return, and we can have fellowship together. I have been thinking about building a church on the riverbank for those of us unwilling to compromise our Christian beliefs and values. You could help me start the church! I have already written some new songs!" Evangelical peered into Pilgrim's eyes hoping for confirmation of his beliefs.

"I need to see the river first. Then I will decide. I have come too far not to get a good look at my destination." With those words Pilgrim strode off with Truthful beside him.

PART 10
THE CELESTIAL CITY

Pilgrim and Truthful turned their backs on Evangelical and walked in silence. Several miles slipped by without encountering anyone. Finally Pilgrim spoke. "What do you make of the things that my friend Evangelical told us?"

"They were disturbing. I have always held that truth is expressed in ideas and concepts. His words made we think I had been wrong all along."

Pilgrim nodded. "I am also distraught over what he said. What is the gospel without doctrines and beliefs? What about the doctrine of the Trinity and the Incarnation? Are they not true? What about the Virgin Birth and the Resurrection? What about salvation by grace through faith? Does this mean that Christianity is not true? Does it mean that other religions are just as valid as ours? Are there going to be Muslims in the Celestial City? I don't know if I could handle that!"

"As I understood Evangelical, it is worse than that. It is not that every religion might be true. It means that that no religion is true. Truth transcends religion and philosophy. I have a hard time getting my mind around that."

"What bothers me most is what he said about the Scriptures. If the Book is not our guide to the Celestial City, then what is? How can we discern truth from falsehood? How will we test spirits? How will we get across the river? It is said that Leviathan swims those waters devouring believers before they reach the other shore. How can we defeat him without the Sword of the Spirit? I understand why Evangelical stayed here."

They continued to walk and discuss the other things that Evangelical had told them. As they traveled the air grew noticeably sweeter and the sun warmer.

"This must be Beulah Land," observed Pilgrim. "I remember reading about it in the Book. At least the Book is still a trustworthy guide on this side of the river."

Birds sang. Their songs declared the glory of the Lord. Flowers bloomed around them. They seemed to proclaim the splendor of the Creator. Soon they came within sight of the River. On either side of the river were trees bearing fruit, twelve different kinds of fruit in their season.

"This must be the River of Life, and these are the Tree of Life, whose leaves are for the healing of the nations."

The river was broad – much wider than any river they had ever seen. In fact it seemed more like a sea than a river. Across the river they could make out the City that was their destination. From the direction of the City they could hear voices of the residents of the City. The voices told of the magnificence of the One who dwells in the midst of the City. Pilgrim's heart pounded. "My heart yearns for that City, like for no other place."

"How shall we get across the river? It is wider than any earthly river, and I am sure it is as deep as it is wide. And I see no vessel which could take us across."

"We must swim it. It will take all our strength... and more. That is for sure. I think we need to get a good night's rest before we attempt a crossing."

So the pilgrims decided to spend the night by the riverside. They made camp. They drank from the river. It was the sweetest water than they had ever tasted. It was more like drinking light than water. They laid down next to the river to sleep. But sleep would not come. For one thing, it did not get dark in that land. It was too close to the City where there is no Night. Perhaps it was also the fruit of the Tree of Life which restored their strength. Or maybe it was because they were so excited to reach their destination. In any case they could not sleep, although they tried their best. They laid down and closed their eyes.

THE BEATIFIC VISION

In that twilight realm between sleep and consciousness Pilgrim dreamed. At least he thought it was a dream, but it may have been a vision. Or it may have been reality. The boundaries between these states were blurred on this Enchanted Ground by the River. He dreamed of a stairway between earth and heaven with angels ascending and descending upon it. He dreamed of wrestling with one of the angels until at long length he received a blessing from him. "What is your name," Pilgrim asked the Wrestler. "You asked me that once before millennia ago, and I would not tell you then. Neither will I tell you now. But to cross the river you must tell me your name – the New Name that no one knows but you."

Pilgrim spoke the Name. When he did, the world dissolved around him. Every event of his life appeared before his eyes simultaneously. He could see beyond his own lifetime to the lives of his parents and grandparents. The vision branched like a tree, and he saw at one glance the lives of all his ancestors. He understood how those lives were connected to the lives of all humans who had ever lived. The Tree branched to include his pre-human ancestors, primates who also bore the image of God.

All of life was One Life, which is the Life of God. Earth was but one small and brief episode of the Big Story. The Story transcended this planet, this solar system, this galaxy, and even this universe. He dropped into the Singularity from which our universe was born, and found himself in the parent universe which spawned our own. From that universe he dropped again into another one that spawned that one. Then there was another. There was universe upon universe. Finally the multiverse collapsed into Eternity. Pilgrim heard music like he had never heard before. It was the Song of Creation. He recognized it as the song sung by the birds and the river. The music flowed over him like water.

Pilgrim was jolted awake by the water. He sat up abruptly, wiped his eyes, and saw his friend Truthful standing over him dripping wet. "Sorry to startle you awake, friend! But you have been asleep for hours and I could not wake you. The only way I could think to arouse you was by splashing handfuls of water on you from the river. It is time to get going."

THE CROSSING

Pilgrim stood up. He did not say a word to Truthful about his vision. He would not have been able to describe what he had seen even if he tried. And he did not want to try. He knew that speaking the vision would have changed it into something completely different. In silence he stepped into the river. Truthful followed. They waded a thousand feet, and it was only up to their ankles. They walked another thousand, and it was up to their knees. Another thousand brought it to their waists. When it reached their chests they had to sink or swim.

"I have a confession to make," said Truthful. "I never learned to swim."

"Now you tell me! Come on. Get on my back. I will carry you," offered Pilgrim without a second thought. "I lost one friend due to my fear and cowardice. I will not lose another, even if it costs me my life."

That is when he remembered words spoken by the Wrestler in his dream: "Whoever seeks to save his life will lose it, but whoever loses his life for my sake will find it."

Pilgrim continued walking with Truthful on his back. When the water grew deeper Truthful climbed onto his shoulders. The water went over Pilgrim's head. He held his breath, and kept walking. He would not abandon Truthful, even if it meant his death. Having seen the birth and death of stars and endless universes, the death of his earthly body seemed unimportant in comparison. All that mattered was that somehow, in some form, he reached the other shore.

Truthful began to squirm and struggle. The water must be going over his head, thought Pilgrim. Then Truthful was off his shoulders. Pilgrim floated to the surface and caught a breath of air. He saw Truthful thrashing in the water beside him.

"Calm down," Pilgrim commanded him. "Lean back and try to float on your back. Stretch out your arms straight and put your hands on my shoulders. Just relax I will swim you to the other shore. We will get there together." But Truthful was in a panic and could not hear a word. He grabbed Pilgrim by the neck, choking him and pulling him under.

He fought with Truthful, wrestling with him under the water. Pilgrim elbowed him in the side and punched at his face to get him to release his grip. "We shall both die here in this River," thought Pilgrim. They wrestled in the dark waters for what seemed to be hours. Words from the Book came to Pilgrim's mind, and he prayed the words as if they were his own:

"I called out to the LORD, out of my distress,
    and he answered me.
Out of the belly of Sheol I cried,
    and you heard my voice.
For you cast me into the deep,
    into the heart of the seas,
    and the flood surrounded me.
All your waves and your billows
    passed over me.
Then I said, 'I am driven away
    from your sight;'
The waters closed in over me to take my life;
    the deep surrounded me;
weeds were wrapped about my head
at the roots of the mountains.
I went down to the land
    whose bars closed upon me forever;
yet you brought up my life from the pit,
    O LORD my God."[33]

HOMECOMING

The water swallowed Pilgrim, and he lost consciousness. When he awoke he found himself sprawled on the river bank. The first thing he did was look around for Truthful. Seeing no one, he concluded that he must have drowned. He fell to his knees and wept.

"I have failed again!" he cried.

Then he heard Truthful's voice. "No, you have been faithful to the end. We have reached our goal. We are on the other shore."

Pilgrim looked around but saw no one. "Where are you, friend?"

"I am with you always, even to the end of the age."

"I hear you, but I do not see you. Where are you?"

"I am within you, guiding you."

"Are you dead?" asked Pilgrim. Pilgrim looked around him. "Am I dead? If I am on the other side, where is the Celestial City? I do not see it."

"It is just over the hill. Walk and see."

Pilgrim walked. On this side of the River there was no path. It was wide and open space. He could smell the fragrance of the Tree of Life. The air was filled with light. The Song of the Universe, which he had heard in his vision, could be distinctly heard. "I am certainly across the River!" He began to run.

He saw a house in the distance. "Perhaps the residents of that humble home can tell me where the Celestial City is," he said aloud.

He ran to the door and knocked. The door opened, and his father stood before him. "Dad, what are you doing here?" From behind his father came the voice of his mother, "Who is it, dear?" Pilgrim's father did not answer. Instead he reached out and gathered Pilgrim in his arms and held him. Pilgrim's mother appeared and likewise embraced her son.

"You have come back!" she cried with tears streaming down her face. "We thought you were dead."

Pilgrim replied, "I have been crucified with Christ. It is no longer I who live, but Christ who lives in me."

"I see you are still religious," his father said. "Well, that is fine. We will not stand in your way. Son, come around to the back so we can talk."

"I will bring you something to eat. You must be famished," his mother said, hurrying to the kitchen.

Pilgrim's father took him to the backyard. "I need to chop some firewood. Care to help?"

Pilgrim smiled. "Sure, dad."

"Great! First, hand me that water bottle over there. I am very thirsty."

Pilgrim carried the water to his father. "I suspect you are thirstier than you realize," Pilgrim replied with a grin.

About the Author

Marshall Davis is a seeker and a pilgrim, much like the main character in this book. If the original book had not been written over 300 years ago, he could claim it as autobiographical. He was baptized as an infant in one of the oldest churches in America, the historic Tabernacle Church of Salem, Massachusetts, which is famous for sending out the first American foreign missionaries.

He grew up in Danvers, Massachusetts, which was originally part of old Salem Village. Danvers is the location of the Salem Village Witchcraft Hysteria of 1692. As a child he used to play in the graveyard of the Nurse Homestead, where Rebecca Nurse, one of the witches convicted in the Salem Witch trials, was secretly laid to rest.

Confirmed in the Congregational Church, by the time he finished Junior High School, Marshall considered himself an atheist and an existentialist. This change of heart was prompted by reading Albert Camus' *The Rebel* when he was 14. After that he read every other existentialist book he could get his hands on. But the quest did not end there.

As a religion major at Denison University, he explored Christian theology more deeply. First he studied the Death of God movement, and then the works of Paul Tillich and Soren Kierkegaard. He cut his exegetical teeth on the works of Rudolf Bultmann. His undergraduate emphasis was the study of World Religions.

Eventually his spiritual quest led him to profess Jesus Christ as Savior, and he was baptized by immersion at the mouth of the Danvers River, where fresh water meets the sea. As a born again evangelical he soon entered the Southern Baptist Theological Seminary in Louisville, Kentucky, earning a Master of Divinity and Doctor of Ministry degree. He was ordained as an American Baptist minister in 1977.

His spiritual journey continued through forty years of pastoring American Baptist, United Methodist, and Southern Baptist churches in Kentucky, Illinois, Massachusetts, Pennsylvania, and New Hampshire. Along the way he studied at the Tantur Ecumenical Institute in Jerusalem, Israel; the Shalem Institute for Spiritual Formation in Washington, D.C.; and the University of Oxford, England, as a visiting scholar.

His theology has developed over the years, as it came in contact with mystics, atheists, and adherents of other faiths. You will meet many of those characters in the pages of this book. Nowadays he spends his days chopping wood and carrying water at his 18th century home in a small New Hampshire village on the edge of the White Mountains. He writes every day, preaches occasionally, plays with grandchildren often, and continues his journey on the Pilgrims' Way.

OTHER BOOKS
BY MARSHALL DAVIS

The Parables of Jesus: American Paraphrase
Version

Thank God for Atheists: What Christians Can
Learn from the New Atheism

Experiencing God Directly: The Way of Christian
Nonduality

The Tao of Christ: A Christian Version of the Tao
Te Ching

Living Presence: A Guide to Everyday Awareness
of God

More Than a Purpose: An Evangelical Response
to Rick Warren and the Megachurch Movement

The Baptist Church Covenant: Its History and
Meaning

A People Called Baptist: An Introduction to
Baptist History & Heritage

The Practice of the Presence of God in Modern
English by Brother Lawrence, translated by
Marshall Davis

The Gospel of Solomon: The Christian Message in the Song of Solomon

Esther

The Hidden Ones

ENDNOTES

[1] Wikipedia, The Pilgrim's Progress, https://en.wikipedia.org/wiki/The_Pilgrim%27s_Progress accessed September 22, 2017.
[2] Soren Kierkegaard
[3] Philip K. Dick
[4] M. Scott Peck
[5] 19th century folk song
[6] Talladega Nights: The Ballad of Ricky Bobby, starring Will Farrell
[7] Charles Haddon Spurgeon
[8] Occam's Razor
[9] Epicurus
[10] Mark Twain
[11] Robert Schuller
[12] Robert Schuller
[13] Robert Schuller
[14] Bertrand Russell
[15] Richard Dawkins, *The God Delusion*
[16] Mother Teresa of Kolkata
[17] Mother Teresa of Kolkata
[18] Job 3:20-26 English Standard Version
[19] Matthew 10:37
[20] Luke 14:26
[21] Luke 18:28
[22] I Corinthians 7:1
[23] Matthew 12:48-50
[24] Isaiah 5:21
[25] Matthew 7:21-23
[26] Exodus 15:3
[27] Isaiah 42:13
[28] Matthew 26:52
[29] Luke 7:9
[30] Matthew 5:38-45
[31] Ephesians 6:17
[32] I Corinthians 13:10
[33] Jonah 2:1-9

Made in the USA
Monee, IL
16 November 2022

17888799R00125